OUTFOXED

The first bullet came close enough for me to smell. Stench of discharged metal, stink of gunpowder.

I threw myself to the ground, rolled over behind a boulder. I'd plucked my Winchester from its scabbard and was in good shape as far as firepower went.

The shooter was up behind a cluster of small boulders. He was sweating me out a little. He hadn't fired for three, four minutes.

I saw the very tip of his black hat move along the top edge of the boulder. The way his hat bobbed, I could tell he was walking on his haunches.

I got ready for him by angling myself on the far side of the boulder. There was a huge, jagged spire of rock near him. This was the only possible place he could shoot from.

All I had to do was wait.

He gave me enough time to play a hand of solitaire.

I wondered what the hell he was up to.

And then I found out.

My friend had another friend. And the other friend had come up behind me.

"I could put a hole the size of a silver dollar in your forehead," he said. "So I'd put the gun down and stand up real nice and easy . . ."

Berkley Books by Ed Gorman

STORM RIDERS
LAWLESS

Lawless

Ed Gorman

BERKLEY BOOKS, NEW YORK

LAWLESS

A Berkley Book / published by arrangement with
the author

PRINTING HISTORY
Berkley edition / May 2000

All rights reserved.
Copyright © 2000 by Ed Gorman.
This book may not be reproduced in whole or in part,
by mimeograph or any other means, without permission.
For information address:
The Berkley Publishing Group, a division of Penguin Putnam Inc.,
375 Hudson Street, New York, New York 10014.

The Penguin Putnam Inc. World Wide Web site address is
http://www.penguinputnam.com

ISBN: 0-425-17432-8

BERKLEY®
Berkley Books are published by
The Berkley Publishing Group, a division of Penguin Putnam Inc.,
375 Hudson Street, New York, New York 10014.
BERKLEY and the "B" design are trademarks
belonging to Penguin Putnam Inc.

PRINTED IN THE UNITED STATES OF AMERICA

10 9 8 7 6 5 4 3 2

To Kim Waltemyer

the beginning

In the beginning God created trains, and then He rested a few days and created train *robbers*. Or so it seemed, anyway.

The farther west the railroads pushed, the more train robbers seemed to flourish. They came in all ages, shapes, sizes, nationalities and skills.

A lot of them had colorful names. "Big Nose" George Parrett. "Dutch" Charley Bates. "Tall Texan" Kilpatrick. Richard "Cyclops" Shanahan.

They developed individual skills, these robbers.

Some were good with explosives.

Some were good at opening safes.

Some were good at keeping the horses ready for a fast escape.

Some were good at scaring the living shit out of passengers.

Train robbing wasn't easy.

A couple of nuns and a blind monsignor could rob a stagecoach.

But a train was a formidable piece of machinery and the railroad barons and their Pinkerton flunkies meant to make robbing one of these magnificent iron beasts a lot of real hard work.

Some people had good reason to rob trains.

The railroad had destroyed their lives by conspiring with local and federal government to cheat them out of land and put down any serious kind of protest.

And the railroad hired the Pinkertons to do anything—anything—that would ensure the railroad got its way.

The Pinkertons planted detectives on trains.

The Pinkertons infiltrated gangs.

The Pinkertons killed in cold blood without mercy or repercussion.

Some of the folks the Pinkertons shot, stabbed, burned and hanged had it coming; but many did not.

If you wanted a good, long, happy life, you stayed on the farm or you clerked at the local general store or you got yourself a nice, soft job with the local post office.

But you sure as hell didn't take up train robbing.

There was a farm kid in Kansas—one Samuel Eamon Thomas Conagher—who grew up wanting to be a train robber. Now, isn't that a hell of a thing? As other boys wanted to be Indian fighters or cavalry men or cowboys, young Sam Conagher wanted to be a train robber.

He filled his foolish young head with tales of the Daltons and Bloody Carl Hermann and, most especially, those holiest of all the sacred and holy outlaws, the James Brothers. Especially young Jesse. Young Sam went around most of the time imagining he *was* Jesse, so much so that sometimes he wouldn't respond when somebody said, "Hey, Sam." Sam wasn't his name. Jesse was.

Young Sam stayed in Kansas until he was sixteen and couldn't take it anymore. One night he crept to the bed where his folks slept and kissed his mother good-bye and touched his father on the shoulder, which was about the most loving contact he'd ever had with the harsh man, who'd loved his Sears catalog plow one hell of a lot more than he loved his brood of eight kids.

He sure didn't miss what he was leaving behind. A cabin that just laid down and spread its legs for every rainstorm and snowstorm and windstorm and hail-storm and tornado that came along. Sometimes he wondered if he wouldn't be drier and safer just standing out on the open prairie. Work that stretched from 4:00 A.M. to late night. No close neighbors and hence no kids to play with, but brothers and sisters who always made fun of him because he was not only the youngest and weakest but also the mooniest, what with all them newspaper stories about train robbers he was always cuttin' out and hidin' in his clothes. He had a strong back and that was about the best you could say for him. A weak mind and a strong back.

Young Sam went to Kansas City. He was a boy with a dream: he wanted to rob a train. He wanted to cinch a red kerchief across his face and pack his right hand with a six-gun and spit those immortal words that always rang in his ears: "If you know what's good for you, Mr. Engineer, you'll open that safe and you'll open it now."

The Mr. Engineer bit was his own addition. He'd put it in there to spice up the rest of the sentence.

He lost his virginity his first night in Kansas City. He had a baby face, and a certain type of woman will always go for a face like that.

"Where'd you get that face, anyway?" the girl whispered afterward. She was a bank teller, ostensibly respectable, but a couple of nights a week she'd drift down to the saloons and pluck herself a man. She knew a neat way to sneak him up the latticework and into her second-story room.

"Huh?"

"You're so cute."

"Aw."

"Look. I went and embarrassed you."

"You sure have big breasts."

"Thanks. I'm kinda proud of them. I ain't pretty. That's for sure. But the men sure seem to like my titties."

"You ever slept with an outlaw?"

"What kind of outlaw?"

"Oh, say, you know, like a train robber or something."

"Well, one guy, I think he was some kind of counterfeiter or something. I think that's why he took me out and bought me this fancy dinner and everything. Like maybe I could help him or something, you know, with his counterfeiting. But a train robber, huh-uh. A train robber'd scare me. They're real violent. Mr. Ahearn at the bank says they should all be strung up and left to rot till the birds get finished eatin' them. How come you asked me about train robbers? You sure ain't never gonna be one with a cute little baby face like that."

"I'd wear a mask."

"Oh, would you, now?"

"And I'd talk real tough."

She giggled. "I'll just bet you would."

"And I'd have this here silver six-shooter with this mother-of-pearl handle. And I'd tell 'em my name was Sam James, first cousin of Jesse."

She put his hand on her breast.

"Why don't you kiss me some more now?"

"You know where I could *meet* any train robbers?"

But she kissed him and shut him up.

The Kansas City newspapers had a lot of classified ads for Men Looking For Work. Carpenters and day laborers and bronc busters and even glassblowers. But not a single train robber. Of course it was ridiculous to think that a train robber would advertise for work, but Sam was getting so frustrated in his search, he started having fantasies about it.

ATTENTION YOUNG MEN WHO WANT TO ROB TRAINS
I'm planning to rob a bank shipment next week
and need an able-bodied assistant, preferably
one who thinks he's Jesse James.
Contact me at PO Box 2737.

Life would be so much easier if only the papers would run ads like that.

A couple of days later, he was wandering in a sunny downtown park when he saw a Western-looking kid reading a train schedule. There was something fierce about the kid. He had black eyes and long, black greasy hair and just about the worst raw red pimply complexion he'd ever seen, the complexion somehow contributing to the downright *sinister* air of this kid.

"You want your face punched in?" the kid said, peering angrily above the top edge of his railroad schedule.

"What?"

"I asked if you wanted your fucking face punched in."

"Why would I want my face punched in?"

"Because you're a hayseed jerkwater asshole who

don't have no better manners than to stand there and gawk at somebody."

"I was just noticin' your train schedule was all."

"Well, you noticed it so shove off."

"What's 'shove off' mean?"

The kid put down his train schedule. "You are one dumb son of a bitch, you know that?"

"I just asked a question, was all."

"'Shove off' means get out of here before I push your face in."

"Oh."

"Well, you gonna get out of here or not?"

He watched a pigeon stepping on some teeny-tiny little pigeon turds. "That train schedule."

"What about it?"

"You ever think of robbin' trains?"

The other kid smiled. "Is that what you are, sonny? A train robber?"

"It ain't what I am," Samuel Eamon Thomas Conagher said most sincerely, "but it's sure what I *aim* to be."

And the funny thing was, the other kid didn't laugh. Just looked at Sam a little harder and said, "Well, I'll be. I'll be."

That was the first time Sam and Earl Cates ever met.

Part One

Part One

Chapter 1

After I killed her, I stayed on the run a year. I stayed in the Territory but as far up in the mountains as I could get.

I felled trees, I swept out barns, I washed dishes, I did anything I could to keep warm and fed and to stay out of sight.

After a while, the whole thing started to fade a bit. The nightmares weren't so bad anymore, and some of my guilt eased up, too. I hadn't meant to kill her. It had been pure accident. Just her luck. Just my luck.

I was working a stage stop, helping out a mean old bastard who'd busted his right leg, when I overheard two passengers talking about the town of Templar.

They got my attention. I liked towns. I'd been a

cowboy from the time I was fifteen till I was twenty. But after that, it was strictly towns. And they made Templar sound awful nice. It was a boomtown, they said. But relatively clean, well run, and lots of work for those who wanted it. They said it was the domain of a man named Rutledge but that he was a decent sort of tyrant. Treat him fair, he'd treat you fair.

And then they used a name that was even more enticing than the town itself: Earl Cates.

If it was the Earl Cates I'd known, he'd done well by himself. Not often an ex-convict ends up sheriff of a town. And I knew for sure he'd been in prison because I'd been in there with him. Yuma, it was. Both of us in there for the same gone-bad bank robbery. Both of us serving ten-to-twenty. Until the night of the riot. Three guards with their throats cut, two others hanged from the gun towers. Earl had the same attitude I did. Even the meanest guards, and there were some beauties, let me tell you, were kinder than the prisoners who ran the place. Guards would never cut off your cock and shove it in your mouth after they killed you the way prisoners did.

Plus, Earl was trying to cure himself of the two things that had put him in Yuma in the first place—liquor and that temper of his. He spent his time reading and quoting the Bible, while I spent my time reading everybody from Sir Walter Scott to Mark Twain. I left prison an educated man.

Anyway, Earl and I got caught up in the riot, mostly running around and trying to look menacing so the other cons would think we were with them. Then we saw that a con way ass over in the corner of the yard had the warden down on the ground and was going to cut out his eyes with a sharpened spoon handle. I stood in front of the con and the warden while Earl cut the con's throat. Then we helped the warden escape out a tunnel.

They put down the riot by dusk. The mayor had us stay in his office, two guards at the door. The word was already out what we'd done. No way the cons would let us out of there alive.

We rode off at dawn. We had carbines, forty dollars each in double eagles, and two good horses.

Two days later, we split up at the river that divides the Territory just about down the middle.

Earl wanted to go west. Just before he rode off, he handed me a small Bible. A lot of the other men would have mocked him. But I knew he was sincere. He had a bottle problem. When he drank he was a monster. But when he was sober, he was one of the most decent men I'd ever known. The trick was for him to stay sober, and he figured the only way he could do that was through the Lord. I wasn't one for religion myself. I didn't *dis*believe, but then again I didn't *believe* either. Earl said he was going to make a new life for himself. For a time there we'd both loved the same woman, a troubled but fetching Irish girl named Callie. He said we should both ride wide of her, especially if we wanted to stay out of prison.

I wanted to go to Kansas. I wanted to see my folks

before they died, not that it did me any good. They'd both passed a couple of years earlier, which explained why they hadn't written in a long time. I'd been eager to read to them, the first in my family to know how to speak the words the eye saw on the page. I read every book in the prison library, and they had some difficult ones there, too.

About six months after that I was in Denver, which is where I saw Callie again. About a year after that, I killed her.

The stage left just after suppertime.

The manager of the stage station told me what he expected me to do before the next stage and I said, "I'll do it for you, Siras. But then I'm leaving."

"Leavin' ? What the hell you talkin' about?"

"Somethin' I need to do over to Templar."

He made a face. "You heard them two passengers talkin' about it, didn't you, kid?"

He always called me kid. It's the baby face. Even at thirty-one, I still look more or less like a twenty year old. If only I felt that young.

Siras had the opposite problem. He was fifty-one and looked eighty, all frizzy white hair and sun-blackened skin and gimped-up arms and legs.

"I know a man there," I said.

"What man?"

"Don't matter what man. I know a man and he can help me."

"Help you do what?"

"Shit, I don't know, Siras, but I sure as hell don't want to spend my life livin' in some stage stop without any company."

"I'm company, ain't I?"

"Not the kind of company I had in mind, exactly."

"Well, just who the hell gonna read to me at night?"

Soon as Siras found out I knew how to read, he showed me his library of dime novels. He was really proud of it. Twenty-three books. All about the West as imagined by some Eastern writer sitting in a hot little room in New York City. Siras loved the covers especially. He'd just pick up a book sometimes and stare and stare and stare at that cover till you thought he might stare a hole right through it.

Every night, I read to him. He was like a kid who needed a bedtime story or a lullaby. We'd sit in rockers down next to the potbelly stove and I'd read and Siras would rock back and forth and listen.

"Somebody'll come along."

"No, they won't. Nobody wants to live out here."

"Well, then, Siras, you know just how I feel."

"And anyway, I can't do the chores."

"Sure you can. I noticed you've been gettin' around pretty good the last couple weeks. But every time you know I'm watchin' you, you start puttin' on a show."

He grinned. "Pussy is what you're after."

"Among other things, yeah. I can't get used to havin' sex with horses the way you can."

"Very funny."

I packed up two saddlebags. He stood and watched me.

"Sure wish I'd learned how to read."

"Sure wish you had, too, Siras."

"I could read them books whenever I wanted to. And not have to kiss some smart aleck's ass."

"I did what I could, Siras." He'd always wanted me to read more than I did.

He followed me to the door.

"What animal you figure on takin'?"

"The calico."

"I knew you would."

"Well, if you knew I would, why'd you ask?"

I was sick of hassling with him. He wasn't a bad sort, I guess. Just cranky from living alone so long.

"There'll be a stage through in a while, Siras. You'll have some company for the night."

"Yeah, but I'll bet there ain't none of them on board knows how to read."

"There's usually a woman or two. Women usually know how to read."

I went down to the rope corral. The sweet smell of horse shit was on the air. It was full dark behind the snow-peaked mountains. If you listened close enough, you could hear the spring runoff feeding the nearby creek. The water would be so cold it'd numb your teeth and so clean it would fill not only your gut but your soul.

I saddled the calico and rode up by the station door.

"I appreciate you givin' me the job and all, Siras."
"Yeah, I s'pose you do."
I could see he was going to start bitching again.
I rode away.

Chapter 2

The first thing I've always noticed about boom-towns is the stench. The folks elected to run the town don't yet have the money or know-how to provide the citizens basic services. There's nobody to regulate the outhouses, nobody to keep people from dumping waste into the streams, and nobody to pick up the garbage. The smell is overpowering, even in the little neighborhoods that spring up around the downtowns. It's like Mexico. You have to be damned careful about drinking the water.

The second thing I've always noticed about boom-towns is the noise. The mines, of course, are the biggest noise. The steam engines, the operating hoists, the mills and the pumps and the cars. Day and night they go, deeper and deeper into the earth. The trains that haul the silver and lead and gold away also make a lot of noise. The town contributes its own share. In the youngest of boomtowns, the saloons and the casinos and the whorehouses go twenty-four hours a day. And they're usually packed.

The nice thing about Templar was that it didn't smell, and the mines weren't all that noisy, their sounds muffled by the foothills that encircled them.

I got to Templar around two P.M. of a soft spring afternoon. I got myself a sleeping room. I found the cheapest barbershop I could and got myself shaved and shorn of both long hair and beard. Then I went back to the boardinghouse and sat in a tub of scalding water for better than a half hour. I went immediately to bed. I woke to the sound of gunfire somewhere in the near distance. But because it was followed by laughter, I knew it was just a couple of drunks with nothing better to do.

I was a little disoriented at first. Felt strange, lost, lonesome, just lying there and listening to all the fun and frolic down in the saloons and casinos.

I rolled myself a smoke and walked over to the window and looked down at the street.

It looked like a holiday of some kind. There were a lot of lights and whores and miners dancing in the middle of the street. There was gunfire but it was all friendly, and there was a short-run stagecoach and a train arriving at pretty much the same time.

Templar was definitely a going concern.

I went back to bed and slept through the night. I had dreams about women who wouldn't let me sleep with

them no matter how much I pleaded. I woke up with a
useless cock in my fingers. It was dawn.

Two eggs, fried potatoes and three flapjacks just the
way I liked them, fried in pork fat and made from
wheat flour. Breakfast. I ate at a café near the depot. A
lot of the customers were train passengers scared they
wouldn't get their breakfast before their train left. The
women who served the food were sweaty and cranky
and I sure couldn't blame them, the way the customers
were hassling them.

I ate at the counter between a dumpy little guy in
a dusty little suit and a big guy with a derby and a
checked suit. It didn't take much to guess he was a
drummer. Wearing his derby inside meant he must
have been real proud of it.

Derby said, "This is one heck of a town, ain't it?"

His voice startled me. It wasn't effeminate. It was
just high-pitched. Like a piccolo out of tune.

"Sure seems to be," I said.

"Never seen a boomtown that was run this well."

"Rutledge won't put up with no guff," the little guy
said. "That's why he hired Earl as sheriff. Rutledge
and Earl both believe in the good book and that's how
they run this town."

"You call him Earl?" I said.

The man nodded. "Most folks do. He's like kin.
Ain't a man in this town Earl ain't helped out in some
way."

"I agree," the man in the derby said. "Course I'm a little prejudiced. He's my stepbrother."

Ham. This was Earl's brother Ham. Earl had talked about him a lot. How all Earl's father had asked him to do was raise Ham right. Ham was several years younger than Earl. He was the only thing the old man had left Earl when he'd died of dysentery.

He shook his head. And when he did so, his derby started to slide. He put an outsize hand quickly to his head to keep it from sliding off. He sure did like that hat of his.

He saw me staring at his head.

He pointed to his derby. "Thirty dollars. Chicago. The finest money can buy." In this grating, piping voice.

The dumpy little man next me laughed out loud, hard and mean.

Ham looked genuinely hurt. Were those actual tears in his eyes? He stood up abruptly, dumping some money on the counter, and hurried out the door, his great height and weight shoving several lesser mortals aside.

"He's a spooky one," the little man next to me said. "Even if he is Earl's stepbrother. That voice. It's a girl's voice."

"It's just high-pitched," I said, feeling sorry for Ham. There wasn't much he could do about his voice.

"Now, you're the kind of clean-cut young man we're looking for. Just by lookin' at you I can see you come from good stock and have stayed on the straight and narrow." He put out his hand. "Del McCourt. I'm assistant manager over to Mr. Rutledge's general store."

"Good to meet you."

"Yes, sir, I can tell you've spent your time on the straight and narrow."

"I've sure tried, sir." Except for the occasional bank robbery and stage holdup. And, oh, yes, that one unfortunate accidental murder I committed.

"The big man who was here," McCourt went on, "he looked like a bent stick, if you catch my drift. That voice of his. I've heard deeper voices on a soprano." Then, "What line of work are you in, Sam?"

I had a story ready. I was good at stories.

"Well, I was a rancher till the banks ran dry last year."

"For that, you can thank the profligates in Washington."

"Wife and two daughters died of cholera on the way out west—the ranch was in Missouri so now I'm not sure what I'll do exactly. Thought I'd look up an old friend of mine."

"Oh? Maybe it's somebody I know."

I mentioned Earl.

"Well, he's certainly just what this town needed, I'll tell you. He brooks no nonsense with the guilty, no nonsense at all."

As he said this, one of the women behind the counter smiled at him.

"My fourteen-year-old boy drank up some corn

liquor one day and smashed out a couple of my neigh-
bor's windows. Earl took him under his wing for a
year and straightened him out. Said he'd been going
bad because he didn't have no pa, was the way Earl
explained it about Mike. Now Mike's workin' in the
mines 'n' doin' just fine."

"Besides Rutledge hisself," McCourt said, "Earl's
the best thing that ever happened to this place."

"I'll tell him you said that."

"No need to tell him. I tell him that myself all the
time."

He slid off the stool and picked up his own derby.
He wasn't much more than five-five and couldn't have
weighed much more than one-thirty.

"Earl be in his office, will he?"

"Should be. He's got two deputies who patrol the
town during the day. That leaves Earl to take care of
the administrative stuff. The Territory's got three new
judges and there's an awful lot of paperwork you gotta
do to help those circuit riders. They ride in and ride out
but they leave all the scut work to the sheriffs and the
marshals."

Then he told me how to find the sheriff's office.

I spent an hour walking around town before I went to
find Earl. The place surprised me. It was a solid town.
There was a whole section of small, neat houses, and
two huge estates, both of which had Victorian-style
mansions sitting on them. There was a steam-driven

trolley and a theater and the largest dry goods store I'd seen in this part of the Territory.

And among all the scruffy, dirty prairie faces you saw rich people, men with top hats and women with bustles and picture hats, being delivered here and there by the same kind of hansom cabs you saw in London and New York. They were like another species. There was a glow about them; and a self-confidence not even drunken gunnies had. They rarely deigned to look about, as if they didn't want their eyesight permanently sullied by all the scrabbling, scrambling, quietly desperate plain folk who packed the streets and the board walkways.

It was a real town, a thriving one, and Earl was its sheriff. And it was sure hard as hell to figure out how he'd ever pulled *that* off.

Chapter 3

The sheriff's office was two stories of brick and bars. Aside from the bank, it was the only brick building in town. Money and law-and-order were the important things here.

Earl had hired himself hard cases. The two deputies who watched me enter the large, open office looked as if they'd recently gotten out of Yuma themselves. They were clean-shaven, they wore fresh khaki uniforms, and their campaign hats were nice and new, but they had the look of serious and competent men.

"Help you with something?" said the one with the scar.

"Looking for Earl."

He smiled coldly. "Most folks around here call him Sheriff. I'm not sure he'd appreciate Earl. Not unless you were kin or something."

"You can tell him it's Sam Conagher."

The other deputy got up and came around the desk and offered his hand. We shook. "Name's Grimes. Sidney Grimes. Hail from Australia originally." And as he said that I heard a little Aussie in his accent. But it wasn't the accent interested me. It was the skin color. He had to have Negro in him.

He saw me looking at him and grinned. "Don't worry. The sheriff didn't go out and hire himself a bunch of jungle bunnies, mate. There's just a speck of aborigine in me is all. If I was dark blood, Ryan here wouldn't work with me. He hates the colored race, he does."

The door in the west wall opened and Earl Cates stood there. He didn't look any fancier than the other two—same uniform, same hat, maybe his star was a little bigger—but he looked a whole lot meaner. He'd picked up a scar and an eye patch and I almost laughed. Earl loved theatrics. The eye patch must've pleased him.

"He called you 'Earl,' Sheriff," Ryan said, sounding like a third-grade snitch.

"He did?" Earl said in his usual sardonic way. "Well, you know what we'll have to do with this bastard? We'll have to take him right out to the town square and hang his ass."

He laughed all the way across the floor. The closer he got, the clearer I could see the gold Christian cross he had pinned to his shirt right next to his badge. He'd been sort of like a preacher in prison. In his own strange way, at any rate.

He slid an arm around my shoulder and said, "I figured you'd be dead by now, Sam."

"Almost made it a couple of times."

A tall man who was able to hide his quickness, his strength and his viciousness well in his easygoing manner, he stood back and looked at me some more.

"You look good, son." He acted happy to see me but he didn't act the least surprised.

"That 'son' stuff still doesn't work, Earl. I'm six months older than you are."

"According to the calendar, son. But not according to what old Earl's got up here." He tapped his temple. "Well, c'mon. Let's make this welcome official. We'll go get something to drink." He smiled at his deputies. "There's a couple of prisoners in the back who haven't had their regular beatings yet today. Take care of them for me, will you?"

That was another thing about Earl. You could never quite decide when he was kidding.

The bartender knew what Earl wanted. Not a word was exchanged. Earl walked up to the bar and the man handed him a small bottle of ginger ale and a glass.

"Gosh, Sam, I can't believe it's you."

"Me? The surprise is you. That badge."

He laughed. "Well, first they wouldn't even let me be a deputy, because of being in Yuma and all. And then they let me be a deputy after I started bein' a part-time preacher over to the Baptist Hall. They started comin' to hear me talk. And then when their sheriff started taking bribes to fix certain things up—I guess they figured I was worth a try. So here I am."

"Still thumpin' the Bible."

"Still tryin' to bring the words of Jesus to the people, Sam. You know how sad and scared most people are down deep? Even the big swaggering ones with lots of money. You get them alone sometime and really talk to them and you'll see they're just like everybody else. They need reassurance that they're living their lives in a good way. And that after they die there'll be another world—a better world waiting for them—and that they had better be preparing for that world now, through prayer and good works."

I watched him. The long sad face. The deep blue eyes that looked crazed sometimes. The long, narrow but rough hands he kept flat on the table as he spoke. In many ways, he was as rough as the frontier. And yet in his sorrow—and his sorrow never quite left him—you sensed his decency, sensed that just about anything you'd gone through, so had he. And maybe he'd even drawn some wisdom from his experiences.

I said, "You really believe there's a heaven?"

"I really do."

"And a hell?"

"There truly is, Sam."

"And that you can change yourself, down deep I mean?"

"I see it happen frequently to those who receive God's word."

It could all be a scam, of course. He was a hell of a good actor. I looked at him there—so serious, somber—and a part of me wanted to laugh. He'd found a whole town that had let itself be taken in.

But I couldn't be quite sure because of those blue eyes and the terrible things they'd seen—things Earl himself had done with his bottle and his fists; and things that had been done *to* him.

"There just may be a job for you," he said.

"That'd be great."

"Nothing permanent. Just something to tide you over till you found some better work. My stepbrother and his friend's doing it, too, matter of fact."

"Doing what?"

"Working at this burned-out mansion. Cataloging things and setting them in boxes to be restored. The fire left everything a big mess."

"I think I could handle that."

"Pay's decent for around here."

"Great. Who do I talk to?"

"I know the owner of the place. I'll set it up for you."

"I'd really appreciate that."

He leaned over and put his hand on my shoulder. "I got a wife and two stepkids now, Sam. I'm appreciating the *really* important things in life. I want to see you have the same things." He lifted his small bottle of ginger ale. "I still have my problems from time to time but mostly I stick to this stuff."

"I appreciate you helping me out, Earl," I said.

"My pleasure, Sam."

The first time I saw the girl, she was just leaving a place called New York Fashions.

This was later in the day. I'd had something to eat and was just wandering around town. All the shops and things made me feel young. I'd spent my late teens and several years of my twenties in Yuma. I'd never had much experience with a really booming town like this one. It all kind've scared me a little and I was surprised when strangers addressed me so friendly and all. I got that old feeling of being ashamed of myself without quite knowing why. I guess I just figured if you got to know me you'd hate me, which was why I stuck with Earl in Yuma. I knew he wouldn't hate me because of what Jesus had taught him and all, about accepting folks even if they were scum.

She wore a long blue belted dress with a prim white collar. Her mahogany-colored hair reached her shoulders and glinted in the sunlight like precious metals. She was probably twenty or so and beautiful, with lively dark eyes and a quick sweet smile and a certain sense of the fragile about her . . .

I couldn't stop looking at her. In fact, I even followed her a few blocks, to where an old Negro waited

for her in a surrey. She set her packages in the back
and then let the man help her into the wagon. She
glimpsed me once and then looked away, distracted by
something more interesting.

I stood and watched her go.

The only other time I'd felt anything like this . . .

I pushed the thought away.

The only other time had been with Callie. And Callie was dead.

I went into a saloon and had a beer. I just kept thinking of the girl, who she was, what she was about. This
kid face of mine—or maybe it's better to describe it as
a mask because that's what it feels like sometimes—
has always helped me with the women.

But she hadn't seemed interested at all.

There was a general store. I bought socks and underwear and a new razor. I also bought a bar of hard
soap. I didn't feel well cleaned unless I used the kind
of soap that rubbed me raw.

I bought a couple of dime novels, too. I thought of
Siras and sort of felt guilty. Cranky old bastard out
there all alone. Nobody to read to him at night. He was
like a kid, he was.

The long ride, the tension of seeing Earl again, and
general fatigue led me back to my hotel room.

There was nobody behind the desk. I took my key
and climbed the stairs.

I got the key in the lock and the door pushed back
and there she was, sitting on the edge of my bed and
looking up at me.

"Hi, Sam," she said in that kind of sweet-sad voice of hers.

The woman speaking was Callie Wilson. The woman I'd killed several years ago.

Chapter 4

I kept expecting to wake up. I kept expecting her to vanish. In dreams, people do that all the time. Just vanish.

But just then the street below got noisy with some cattle being run into a chute over by the depot. And a fly landed on my left cheek and triggered a tic. I felt sick to my stomach. None of this was the stuff of dreams. Way too real.

I walked over to the bureau and set down the stuff I'd bought.

I rolled a smoke. I didn't know what else to do. I didn't know what to think or say or feel.

I kept my back to her. But we could see each other in the mirror above the bureau. You think of whores and heartbreakers as being flashy or trashy, I suppose. But Callie had always dressed quietly in prim suits and

cute little hats. Her fierce red hair was the only extrav-
agant thing about her. It was sparkling, gorgeous,
tucked under the robin's egg blue hat that matched the
robin's egg suit she wore.

"Earl said you'd probably kill me for sure this time.
If I surprised you this way."

"Am I supposed to laugh, Callie?"

"I'm sorry about everything, Sam. The way I treated
you and all."

I saw the rosary in her hand. It was funny, her and
Earl being so religious and all. She used to drag me to
church to light candles with her and pray that she
wouldn't be unfaithful anymore. She'd known Earl
when she was real young and they'd lived together for
a time and he gave her up because he couldn't take her
cheating on him. He told me he was afraid he'd kill her
some night. Still, I think he was jealous of me when *I*
hooked up with her. He never said anything but I think
it helped him in some way to see that she cheated on
me the way she'd cheated on him. People think like
that sometimes. She was a whore and she wasn't a
whore. Or maybe I should say she was a whore but she
paid for it. Inside, I mean. Nobody could hate Callie
worse than Callie. All you had to do was look at her
wrists. At how many times she'd slashed them. She almost died on me a couple of nights there when I
walked out after she fucked somebody else—always
some rich guy, Callie hating rich people and at the
same time *wanting* to be rich—and finding her there
unconscious and near dead and picking her up and

running her to the nearest doc's. You couldn't trust
Callie. But the worst thing was that *Callie* couldn't
trust Callie.

I watched her in the mirror. "The last time I saw
you, you were dead."

"You ran away too fast. You just *thought* I was dead.
You were scared, I guess. Anyway, this very nice
young man came along and saved me. Got me breathing and throwing up."

"Sorry I missed it," I said. "How'd you meet up
with Earl?"

"I heard he was in town here. I decided to come see
him. He's turned out real good." She paused. "I think
about our baby all the time."

"It wasn't a baby. It was just a mess of blood."

She'd miscarried one night while I was sleeping. I
woke up and the blood was all over my legs and stomach. She wasn't right in the head for two, three
months. She'd wanted that kid pretty bad. So had I, I
guess.

"I guess I still think of it as a baby. A person."

I'd bought a bottle of rye. I poured myself one.
There was only one glass. I gave it to her and drank
out of the bottle.

I took a chair and sat down across from her.

She looked so vulnerable and hurt. It's funny, some
of those are the ones you really have to watch out for.
They have to keep trying to compensate for the grief
they've had all their lives, and somehow in the process
you get destroyed.

"Earl says we're going to work together."

"Aw, shit."

"I won't bother you any, Sam. I promise."

I couldn't help myself. "How many men you fucked in the last month, Callie?"

The brown eyes registered sudden sharp pain. I felt, in equal parts, good and bad about how I'd stunned her. Quietly, she said, "I try not to do that so much anymore, Sam."

"What, you just give 'em blow jobs now?"

Then I felt like hell. "I shouldn't've said that, Callie."

"It's all right. I know I got it coming, Sam."

We sat quiet for a couple minutes. Didn't drink. Didn't talk. Just sat and looked at each other most of the time.

It was strange, being in this room with her. I could see the dust in the slash of sunlight and hear the faint roll of the player piano from down the street. Everything was so real and yet here I was talking to a dead woman.

"I almost had another one, Sam."

"A kid?"

"Yes."

"What happened?"

"Same thing."

"I'm sorry."

"Yeah. So'm I."

"You're young yet, Callie," I told her.

"I don't feel young. And I bet you don't either."

"Nope. I guess I don't."

"I figured you'd be settled down by now."

"Didn't have time for that," I said. "I was on the run for murdering a woman."

"Oh, gosh, Sam. I'm so sorry. I just figured you knew I was alive."

We were quiet again. She finished her drink. I passed the bottle her way. She shook her head.

"You know his stepbrother?" I said.

"Yeah."

"What's his story?"

She shrugged. "A daydreamer. Like us. He's in love with me, he says. I feel sorry for him."

I smiled. "If he's really in love with you, I feel sorry for him, too."

She laughed. She had a nice easy girly laugh. "Thanks a lot." She stood up. "I'd really like to kiss you, Sam."

"No, thanks."

"It'd be just a friendly kiss. I really did love you back then."

"Yeah, that's what you said anyway."

She went over to the battered bureau and set her empty glass down.

"Well, I guess I better get back to my room."

I stayed in my chair.

At the door, she said, "So long, Sam."

"Yeah," I said. "So long."

Chapter 5

There were two mansions. Well, one-and-a-half, actually. The new Victorian was in front and a few hundred yards behind it stood the blackened remains of the old one.

On a sunny morning like this one, the old house looked like a cutaway diagram. You could see how the house had been organized, the winding staircase climbing three full stories, the wallpaper patterns of various rooms, even how the heating pipes had snaked throughout the house.

The new house was still being worked on. Several wagons filled with lumber and kegs of nails and shingles for roofing and rods for draperies. Men in shirt-sleeves carrying hammers and levels and screwdrivers and saws. Horses being turned back to town to pick up

more supplies. Busy. And no slackers. Everyone working hard. Not even any chitchat.

The wagon that had let off Callie and me was just
now swinging back toward town.

"How'd you like to live here, Sam?"

"Guess I could get used to it."

She leaned in. "I still don't like rich people. They
think they're so special. The way they treat people like
us."

"I wouldn't mind being one of them."

She laughed. "I'll bet you wouldn't."

We'd been told to ask for a Mr. Proctor.

He was standing in front of the remains of the old
mansion. He looked like a New England school-
teacher. Prim, proper, prissy in his dark suit and white
collar.

"Good morning," he said.

We nodded hello.

"You must be Callie and you must be Sam."

He had a nice voice, surprisingly so. The voice
didn't belong with the getup or his somewhat cultured
and pained face.

We shook hands. He could have beaten me easily at
arm wrestling. I decided I liked him. He wasn't a prig,
after all.

"Why don't I walk you around the house and show
you how it's working?"

We followed him around. He spent a good twenty
minutes patiently showing us what to do. In the ashes
and crevices and rubble were all kinds of trinkets and

artifacts that the crashing wood had smashed and hidden.

Four workers—two men, two women—now walked among all the debris, carefully looking for anything that looked "useful, important, intriguing or questionable"—"questionable" meaning we should consult him before we decided its worth.

One of the women found a doll's head while we watched her. A little later, one of the men found a railroad watch.

He then showed us the tablet that was kept from flying away by a large rock. When we found something worthwhile, we were to write down a description of it on the tablet. Then set the item in the box nearby. Not exactly a brain-taxing task.

"Didn't the sheriff say his stepbrother would be coming, too?" Proctor said to Callie.

"He should be along."

"Well, no sense waiting. Why don't we get to work?"

He gave us pencils and white cotton gloves to put on.

This wasn't exactly the kind of work I was used to. But the pay was good and it would supplement my meager bankroll.

The stepbrother didn't show up for another two hours.

I recognized him right away.

The derby. The checkered suit. And the high-pitched, irritating voice raised in greeting Callie.

By this time, we were pretty sooty from the ashes. Ham, as she called him, didn't look eager to shake my hand. Proctor had already given him his white cotton gloves to put on. He wanted his own dirt on them, not mine.

"I've heard a lot about you from Earl," Ham said as he took his place next to us.

Proctor came over and said, "We don't talk as we work, Mr. Damon. That's the rule, I'm afraid."

He said it pleasantly enough. No bully. No prissiness. Just a fact.

"Cocksucker," Ham said as Proctor turned and walked away.

The word sounded funny in a voice that high.

I guess because of the voice, I'd dismissed Ham yesterday as flowery, if not an outright flower. But I saw now I was wrong. There was great power in the beefy shoulders and chest. The knuckles beneath the thin layer of white cotton looked twisted. He'd busted them many times, had our Ham.

Then he finally got down to serious work.

Every once in a while he'd look up to glare at Proctor's back. It was easy to imagine him sliding a knife into it.

The morning was long. For a time I'd keep looking at my railroad watch. It was never more than three or four more minutes later than the last time I'd looked. I hated work like this. You chased down strays, you chopped timber, you hauled water to slop the pigs, you

baled hay, you rode fence—the time went along pretty
good.

But not this kind of work.

Proctor came over and said we could take a break. I
hadn't realized how sore my back was until then. The
bending over was hard on the muscles.

There was a well up near the barn. A bunch of workers were standing around it. When they saw Callie
they started nudging each other and smirking.

She had this way of pretending not to pay any attention to men at all. And they loved it. They'd tease her
and whistle and laugh, anything to catch her attention.
She monitored all this from the corners of her emerald
green eyes.

"You want some water, Callie?" Ham said.

The other workers hadn't heard him talk before.
They stopped paying attention to Callie. Now they
were all caught up in Ham. What he sounded like, I'd
figured out, was one of the ventriloquist acts you see
in theaters. The little guy sits on the big guy's knee and
speaks and it's usually in this high-pitched voice. It's
not a nancy voice, really, it's more of a little kid's
voice.

But it sure was fascinating to these workers.

Now they were nudging and poking each other
again, but it was because of Ham. Callie was momen-
tarily forgotten.

I saw it taking shape.

One of the workers, the boldest, stepped away from
his chums and walked up to Ham.

Flounced up to Ham, was what he did, in that high-stepping mincing way in which men always imitate women.

It was funny, what was on Ham's face. You might think there'd be anger there. Or contempt. But there was just sorrow.

And I figured I knew why.

He was weary of it. All his life, people'd made fun of him because of his voice. There was nothing he could do about it, not unless he wanted to go live in a cave somewhere.

I felt sorry for him. I guess I'd kinda felt the same my whole life, too. There was always trouble, it seemed. A lot of it was my own fault. But some of it just happened to me. A part of me just wanted to rest. To never have to face another confrontation again. And that went quadruple for Ham, I imagined. He'd want just one day in his life when somebody didn't make fun of his voice.

He said, "You get back over there."

They all laughed, of course. That keening voice. Trying to order this curly haired, muscle-bound, grinning worker around.

"I've never fought a girl before. This'll be fun."

"I'm warning you."

More laughter.

Ham was big, wall big, wall wide, wall tall. His fists were like clubs. But still, the smaller man had an air of the killer about him. There are some men who just like to fight. And he looked to be one of them.

He hitched up his Levi's and rolled up the sleeves of his long underwear.

"Any time you're ready, Miss Nancy."

"One more time. I'm warning you."

"And one more time, I'm warning *you*. I won't go to the dance with you next Saturday night."

Oh, his chums loved that one. They were a real sophisticated audience, they were.

And then Ham hit him.

He hit him with an uppercut that lifted the worker a good foot off the ground. And before the man had time to hit the ground, Ham hit him five or six more times. The man started bleeding from his eyes, his nose and his ears.

It couldn't have taken six seconds.

The man lay twisting and twitching in the dust.

A man started to lunge for Ham but I had my gun out and waved him off.

The worker started going into some kind of spasm. It was pretty ugly to watch.

One of them waved a bucket at me. I nodded *all right*. He pumped the bucket full and then threw it over the man on the ground.

The water helped some, enough to revive him anyway.

He kept saying, "What happened to me? What happened to me?"

You see that in prizefights sometimes. A man is beaten so quickly and badly that he loses all memory of it forever. I suspected that would be the case here.

They helped him to his feet. He was shaky. They supported him and started walking back toward the road.

I hadn't paid any attention to Ham. He was sitting on the edge of the well, ladling water over the knuckles of his right hand.

"You all right?"

He raised his eyes. They were sad again. "Just leave me the fuck alone."

"Hey. That's some nice talk."

"You heard what I said." He shook his head. "No wonder she can't fall in love with me."

"Who?"

"Callie. People always makin' fun of me. Who could love somebody people're always makin' fun of? Fuckin' voice. Sometimes, I think I'd rather be mute than have a fuckin' voice like this one."

"You ever seen a doc?"

"Oh, I seen plenty of docs. You know what one of them said to me?"

Apparently, he'd forgotten about chasing me away.

"What?"

"Said maybe I could get a job in a circus." He spat in the dust. "Fuckin' docs."

"I'd say you should take up boxing. You're scary to watch."

"I don't like it. It hurts my knuckles." He held up his left hand for me to see. The knuckles were swollen and red. Then he shook his head. "Plus I nearly killed a guy one time. Came this close to hangin'. He was out of it for three weeks. Then he came to and he was good as new so they let me go." He looked down at his knuckles. Then up at me. "I ain't nancy."

"I didn't think you were."

"Most people, on accounta my voice, they think I am. But I ain't." The sad eyes again. "Though sometimes I wish I was."

"I never heard anybody ever say that before. That they wished they were a nancy."

"It's on account've Callie."

"Oh."

"I'm in so much pain all the time, I just wish I was anybody except me. Even a nancy'd be better than this."

Most men, they didn't talk like this. They didn't just tell you what they were feeling. You sort of had to guess it, read it between the lines.

But not Ham.

"You lived with her, huh?"

"Yeah."

"She talked about you sometimes."

"I'll bet she did."

"No, sometimes she said nice things. Other times—"

"I got sick of her running around on me," I said.

"I guess she never mentioned that."

"She wouldn't."

"You sound kinda bitter."

"I'm not the right one to ask about Callie."

"I just don't know what to do, I love her so fucking much."

Proctor was there, then.

He said, "Back to work, gentlemen. And, Ham, we
don't encourage fighting around here. Just for the
record."

But Ham wasn't listening. I could tell by his gaze he
was still thinking about Callie.

On the way back I told Callie I felt sorry for him.

"So do I."

"He isn't a nance."

"I didn't say he was."

"He loves you."

"I know he does. I wish he didn't. For his sake."

I thought of all the nights I'd lie awake for her. I
used to pray she'd come home. Pray as hard as I could,
usually with her rosary wrapped around my fingers.
And she'd come home all right, drunk and mussed up
and stinking of sex. And then I'd pray that I could pull
away from her somehow. But I never could; I never
could.

The afternoon went pretty much like the morning. I
started looking at my watch again. Five o'clock
seemed weeks away.

Every time I'd look over at Ham, he'd be watching
Callie. Callie didn't seem interested in either one of
us. She was Proctor's best worker.

After a while, I figured out why.

She'd find something that interested her—some
keepsake or icon—and stick it in her full skirt. Callie
was working hard, all right. For Callie.

Around two the singing started. It was beautiful. It wasn't my kind of singing—it was fancy stuff—but the voice was like a dream of a woman you have sometimes, just a daydream about a woman who is so lovely and graceful and gentle that she probably couldn't ever exist. But it was in this girl's voice, that daydream quality, and it gave me the honest-to-God chills.

"God, she's got a beautiful voice," I said at break time.

Callie said, "Some rich bitch." Callie had a prairie girl's hatred of rich people. She didn't mind taking rich men for their money but inside she despised them the whole time. She was almost saintly in some ways; in others she was ruthless.

"Nora Rutledge," Ham said.

Ham, who had just stopped working, stared at the house just as the singing stopped. Then he did something strange. He took out this little notebook from the back pocket of his checkered drummer's pants and wrote something down.

I wondered what he was writing about.

The man Ham had worked on looked bad. The whole side of his face was puffy and bruised and you could see spiderwebs of blood in both of his eyes.

He tried to glare at Ham but it was almost sad. He couldn't even *fake* being tough anymore.

The singing girl was on the front porch then.

She was just as pretty as her voice. I knew girl and song were the same. They had to be.

She was the same dark-haired girl I'd seen in town. The one Ham had written something down about.

She wore jodphurs and a white blouse and long brown leather riding boots. A stable man brought a big pinto around to the front of the house and she mounted it and rode off.

I felt the same as I had in town. She set me off. Addled me. Sight of her beat me up just as violently as Ham had beaten up that smart-mouth bastard.

Callie had come over to stand next to me.

"I told you she'd be some rich bitch."

I could feel her looking at me. She laughed.

"Oh, God, Sam, you're crazy if you've got any thoughts about her. She wouldn't let you scrape off her boots."

Ham was writing something in his notebook again. This girl sure seemed to inspire his literary side.

She came back near quitting time.

She looked hot and tired. But still elegant and lovely, still an unreal daydream.

She stabled the horse and then walked up toward us.

I was so nervous as she approached, I kept swallowing to get some saliva in my mouth. In case I had to talk.

She stood at what had formerly been the entrance to the old mansion and said, "I'd just like to thank all you people for doing such a great job. You found so many valuable things yesterday." She was talking about the people who'd started a day earlier. "And I'm sure the new people are doing just as well."

I wanted her to look at me and I didn't want her to look at me. If she looked at me, she'd dismiss me like just some other yokel and drifter, and I didn't know if I could handle that.

"I'm not a very good cook but I did bake a cake this morning. I also made some lemonade and I'd like to share them with you at quitting time."

After she left, Callie put her hand on her hip and strutted around like a princess. She even put on a bit of a British accent. She was good at things like that. "Isn't it grand of me to invite the riffraff in for some tea and crumpets? I'm such a divine lady, aren't I?"

"She's just being nice," I said.

Callie looked at Ham and said, "Sam's in love."

"Cupid's arrow," Ham said.

"Yes," Callie laughed. "He thinks he's got a chance with her."

I just shook my head.

We finished up the day. I found books, smoking pipes, hairbrushes, spurs, whooping cough elixirs, a capote and some Number Six cologne for men which claimed right on the bottle that this had been "President Washington's favorite manly scent." It also cost as much as I'd make in three days' work out here.

I carried everything to the boxes and then catalogued everything in the tablet.

• • •

I went over to the well and washed up. I'd seen Nora put out soap and towels. I damned near took a full bath, I got cleaned up so well. I even snuck over to the box and got myself a little bit of Number Six cologne. I figured if it was good enough for old George, it should be good enough for me.

Callie and Ham didn't spend much time at the well. They mostly washed their faces and hands. The other four did about the same.

Nora had set a nice-looking table. Fresh linen spread, two big pitchers of lemonade and a two-layer cake with white frosting right in the middle of the table.

Nora cut slices for everybody, then served them on saucers. They were fancy saucers, just as fancy as the forks and napkins that went along with them. Even her glasses were fancy, with gold leaf around the middle.

Everything was pretty awkward at first. She was the boss man's daughter. You had to be careful of what you said.

She seemed just as strained as we did, unsure of what to say to us. You could tell she hadn't ever spent much time with working folks.

Me, personally, I didn't care about any of it. I just wanted to watch her.

I kept looking for a flaw. I wanted to find something that would break her grip on me. But there weren't any flaws. And I didn't know if her grip on me could *ever* be broken.

For a time, everybody else just fell away. There was

just Nora and me and the big new mansion behind us. This was every cornball prairie boy's dream—a girl like this, a house like this, a leisured, gentleman's life like this. Callie would never understand it. There wasn't enough danger and excitement in it. She'd get bored quick. And she'd hate all the people. She'd resent them for not having had to live her life.

When I came back to reality, I heard Nora say, "You're sure a quiet one." She looked at me as she spoke. "Everyone's introduced himself except you."

I felt my cheeks get hot. I've never liked to be singled out. It always embarrasses me, people staring at me and all.

"Sam Conagher."

"Conagher. That's a Northern Ireland name. We vacationed there a couple of years ago. It was beautiful and there were a lot of Conaghers."

I didn't know what to say.

Ham said, "You take to horses pretty good, Miss Nora."

"Oh, I love horses."

"So you ride every day."

"Every day I can. First, my singing lessons, and then my ride. That's how I spend most of my afternoons."

Callie sat there resenting her, hating her. For somebody who lied as much as she did, Callie's face didn't keep secrets very well.

"How far do you ride?" Ham said.

"Oh, usually up to that Indian mound in the

foothills. I'm writing an article for the Territory news-paper on the Indian mounds around here. Sometime, I'll have a photographer get some pictures of them."

"You stop and see them every day?" Ham said.

I wondered why he asked so many questions. I also wondered what he'd been writing in that little note-book of his.

"Just about every day. They really evoke the past for me. They help me understand what this land was like before the whites got here." Then, "How's the cake, everybody?"

Great, fine, excellent. You know all the words you use when somebody asks you a question like that.

It wasn't great but it wasn't bad. She probably wouldn't ever be a chef but this tasted fine for a work-day. As did the lemonade, which was just the slightest bit sour.

A breeze came. I closed my eyes and let it seduce me. I could smell the heat of the dying day and the roses and the gladiolas and the petunias and the pines up in the foothills. A fella'd have to be crazy not to want this life out here. And with a woman like Nora to come home to every night. I could see her holding a baby, rocking it, singing some old Irish folksong to it. She'd be as beautiful and fresh as the infant.

A clatter of dishes. When I opened my eyes, people were setting their glasses and silver on their plate. The festivities were over.

• • •

He came around the far side of the house. He wore a big white Stetson, a fancy blue bib-front shirt and a pair of Colts strapped low across his hips. He looked like the kind of cowboy you see on orange crates. No cowboy ever looked that dramatic or clean-cut. But he did. He had Nora's black Irish looks but none of her grace or charm. Even from a couple dozen feet away, the way he moved, the face he made, you could see what an unhappy and agitated fellow he was.

"I hate to interrupt your little party here," he said to Nora, "but aren't you supposed to be getting ready for dinner tonight?"

"I know what I'm going to wear," Nora said, flustered by his accusation. "I've already laid it out."

"This is the governor's brother," he said. "Do I have to remind you how important this dinner is to Dad's business?" He looked at us. "Now, you people get the hell out of here. I don't mean to be rude but my sister's very busy right now."

Nora was angry now. "This is my brother, Cal. Some people think he's arrogant and pushy. I don't know where they'd ever get an idea like that, do you?"

He slapped her.

I automatically started for him.

He slapped her and I grabbed his wrist. He was about three inches taller and thirty pounds heavier but I had surprise on my side.

I twisted his wrist hard so he'd remember this moment.

Nora grabbed my arm.

"Please, Sam, you'll just make it worse."

I let go of his wrist.

He came right back at me. He shoved me backwards. The back of my knees bumped against the seat of the picnic table. He was strong and quick.

I went at him again and she got between us.

Then Ham got between us, too.

"C'mon, Cal," he said. "You just need to calm down a little."

It took a few minutes. I made some fighting noises and so did he. But we let them have their way.

"Nora, I never want to see him on our land again. Do you understand?"

"Yes, Cal."

"I don't know why you had to put on this little spread for them anyway. We pay them good wages and that's enough."

"Yes, Cal."

He came over to me.

"You see me in town, friend, you'd better walk wide. Especially if I've had a few drinks."

"I might say the same to you."

"You might, huh?"

"C'mon, you two," Ham said and got in between us again.

Cal turned away and stalked up to the house.

Nora said, to everybody, "I'm sorry about this."

Everybody responded as they had to her cake. Saying the right things, the proper things. Oh, it's nothing to be embarrassed about, brothers and sisters are always arguing. He was probably just worried about your dinner tonight. Maybe he'd just had a few snorts and was a little owly, was all. And so on.

"Well, thank you, everybody," Nora said. "I guess I'd better get inside now."

We all waved and she started up to the house.

The wagon for town had just pulled into sight.

Nobody said anything as we walked to the wagon. We wouldn't want her to think we were talking about her behind her back. In case she was watching us.

In the wagon, it would be different. In the wagon, there'd be plenty said. Plenty. I heard her call my name. At first, I couldn't see her. Then I saw a small, screened-in porch on this side of the house. The screening was so dark, it made everything on the porch impossible to see.

"You go on ahead," I said to the others.

"Cupid calls," Callie said.

I went over to the porch. She opened the door. Stood on the threshold.

"I don't want Cal to see us. I have to speak quickly."

"All right."

"I'm sorry about today."

"Oh, that's all right."

"And now you're out of a job. Because of me."

This close to her, alone with her, my whole body felt weak. I wanted to be absorbed into her. I'd never felt like this before. Not even with Callie in the early days. It was terrifying.

"I'll be fine."

"You really can't come back here. He has a terrible temper."

I grinned. "Yeah, I kind've sensed that."

"You look so young, Sam. Except for your eyes." She touched my shoulder. "I'm so sorry for all this, Sam. I really am."

I heard her name called from deep within the huge house. Not Cal. A different male voice. Maybe her father.

"Good luck to you," she said. And she was gone.

I was in a daze for the next twenty minutes.

When I came to, I was on the swaying, laboring wagon and night was falling and the lights of town were like fragile flares in the dusk.

Chapter 6

The next morning, I went back to work I liked better. There was a company that paid thirty-five cents for every railroad tie you cut from their timber. They had a good supply of chopping axes and broadaxes and pickaroons and tie peelers. Some companies don't give you much to work with. I got into the rhythm of it and the day went fast. A lot faster than picking trinkets out of a gutted mansion, anyway.

For a week I kept to the same pattern. Work till night, have a good meal in town and drink just enough to get sleepy. I wanted to forget everybody, Nora included. I figured I'd build up some money and light out again.

I didn't know what Callie and Ham were up to. I avoided the places they liked.

I had dreams of Nora. Kid dreams, stupid dreams. I

was always rescuing her from something. She was drowning or Indians were after her or she was in a dark house where a man with a knife was following her up the stairs.

She was always grateful, of course. And so was her old man. He said I was too good for hacking tie from lodgepole pine. He said he had a spot for me in business. And then we were getting married. You know how dreams are. They don't make a lot of sense sometimes.

Her brother Cal was never in the dreams to spoil them. Maybe he'd done all of us in dreamland a favor and stuck a .45 Colt in his mouth.

Most of the men I worked with cutting ties were Polish and didn't speak English. This gave me plenty of time to daydream without being interrupted. Every once in a while, a couple of them would go at it, and hard, too. I never understood their words well enough to know what they were fighting about. One of them who could speak English pretty good said that in a saloon fight the other night a friend of his got the tip of his nose bitten off. He said the man was afraid he'd never have sex again. A guy uglied up that way, not even a whore would want him.

The fourth day a guy had two fingers chopped off. He was pretty bloody. I had to cinch it up for him. He was too hysterical to help. He kept praying in Polish and it was pissing me off, the way he kept keening the same words over and over. He was driving me crazy.

On Sunday, I saw her. Nora. In town. Coming out of

church. A tall, imposing, silver-haired man walked next to her. You could tell the way everybody kind of paid him due that he was her rich-man father.

I guess I kind of arranged it. The big Presbyterian church was where the well-to-do went. I just happened to be walking by there about the time the services were letting out. The truth was, I'd *been* walking by—back and forth—for a little over a half hour.

She wore a brown dress that only enhanced the mahogany colors of her hair and eyes. She glided down the stairs.

You could see the eligible young men gathering together to greet her in the sunshine. Derbies doffed; wide smiles affixed on their faces.

I wanted to be one of them. Have their clothes. Their manners. Their backgrounds. Their futures.

And then I saw Ham.

He was up the street, leaning against a tree in front of a store. He looked relaxed, even a little bored. But I could see the way he watched her. And wrote in his pad.

I wondered again what the hell he was writing.

Nora's father had his own crowd of jittery folks. They owed him money or wanted a favor from him or figured it was just good business to play a game of slave-and-master. The wives might not like to see their menfolk demean themselves this way, but they'd understand that it was necessary.

A hansom cab appeared, driven by a black man in a black suit and top hat.

Nora had disappeared inside her circle of admirers. She seemed to be drowning, in fact.

Her father called her name. The circle broke. The young men wouldn't want to displease Papa.

When she was in the hansom, she leaned forward and waved good-bye to her courtiers. Once, she seemed to raise her eyes and see me. But then she quickly looked away.

Papa was in the cab now. The black man whispered to the horse and the horse quickly pulled away.

I was agitated the rest of the day.

I didn't want to eat or drink. Around nightfall I tried a whore. She got me up all right but I never did come. She probably had lockjaw by the time she was done. I paid double her price.

The rest of the night I lay in bed having daydreams about rescuing Nora.

That was the only way I'd ever get her to even look at me as a true human being. Do something dramatic. So dramatic even her father would have to accept me.

But that was a little boy dream when he's stuck on the freckled girl who sits in front of him in the schoolhouse.

The next day at work I wasn't worth a damn. Too tired. Almost groggy.

She stayed with me, like a ghost. Tender words I could never say out loud. Need gnawed at my chest.

The wagon that brought us back to town passed by the hospital on its way.

It wasn't like a city hospital, such as the one in Denver—two, three stories, with lots of windows, and a small army of white-dressed nurses and somber-faced doctors.

This one was a converted storage facility that one of the railroads had abandoned and given to the town. It was now painted white with HOSPITAL written in red letters on the sides and front of it.

I wouldn't have thought anything of it but I'd learned that Nora worked here two afternoons a week. We'd gotten back early today. She might still be there.

But why would I need to go to a hospital?

I pitched myself off the back of the slow-moving wagon and watched it disappear around the bend that marked the beginning of the town limits.

I stood there feeling hot and tired and stupid. Even if she was in there, what would I say to her? You don't just walk up to a woman of her breeding and start talking to her. You have to have a *reason*.

I was reaching into my shirt pocket for the makings when my elbow touched the handle of my Bowie knife. I always carry a scabbard with a Bowie in it when I work in the forest. You never know.

Now, that would be the kind of thing a fella would have to see a pretty nurse about.

I went over to the side of the road, sat on a rock and smoked my hand-rolled, figuring out where to cut myself.

Along the side of my left hand, I guessed. The meaty part.

It'd bleed like hell and look bad but I wouldn't have to cut too deep.

Be a funny thing if I went to all this trouble and she wasn't even there. But oh God did I want to see that girl. I had to take the chance.

I'll tell you one thing. It hurt a hell of a lot more than I thought it would.

When the blood started coming good and fast, I picked up the piece I'd torn from my work shirt and wrapped it around the wound.

But it looked too fresh.

I rolled the bandage in the dirt. Much better.

I stood up and started for the hospital. I walked slowly, in case somebody was watching me, and I kept shaking my hand as if it stung a lot.

The place smelled of medicine. There was a big room with six or seven chairs. On the wall were three or four posters about docs and health. The bell over the door kept tinkling.

A stout woman in a mother hubbard appeared.

"Afternoon."

"Afternoon, ma'am." I held up my wound like a tyke who wanted it kissed by his mommy. "Afraid I cut myself."

"Let's see."

She came over and looked it over.

"I think you'll probably live."

"Well, that's good to know," I laughed.

"I'll go get the doc."

"Oh, no," I said, too fast. "Not the doc."

She looked at me strange.

"Why not the doc?"

"See, I know one of your nurses here and I'd be a lot more comfortable with her."

"And who would that be?" She looked a lot bigger and tougher suddenly. And a lot more suspicious.

"Uh, Miss Nora Rutledge."

"Nora? She isn't a nurse. She's just a helper."

"Well, whatever she is, she could do a good job of patchin' me up. I'm sure of it."

"You're sure of it, huh?"

I nodded.

Then she smiled.

"You must really want to see her."

I could feel myself blushing.

"Cutting yourself so you could come in here like this."

"I didn't cut myself, ma'am."

"Course you didn't."

"It was an accident."

"Course it was. And she don't even put in that many hours. I mean, we're very appreciative of what she *does* put in, but she might just as easily be at home this afternoon."

"*Is* she at home?" I said, feeling sick and kind of panic-like that I wouldn't get to see her.

She patted my cheek.

"Don't worry, sonny. She's here."

"You won't tell her, will you?" I asked.

"Tell her what?"

"About me cutting myself."

She grinned slyly. "I thought you told me it was an accident."

I was blushing again.

Then she leaned forward. "I won't tell her. You just go over there and sit down."

"Thanks. I appreciate this."

"I'm only doing it 'cause you've got that baby face just like my cousin Neal. And I can't resist baby faces."

There was one interesting wall poster. It showed a doc's bag then listed everything he carried around in it: bismuth, Dover's Powder, morphine, bromide of potassium, compound cathartic pills, podophyllin, tincture aconite, mercury with chalk, calomel, tincture belladonna, fluid extract of ergot and tincture hydrastis. And a case of instruments that included a fever thermometer and obstetric forceps. He had to make sure that all his medicines and instruments fit into his saddlebags.

I tried to sit down but I couldn't.

Not for long anyway.

I'd sit down and then I'd jump right back up again and start pacing.

Oh, I was going to make a fool of myself. I could just see her flying from the room, all insulted and angry over my stupid trickery.

It seemed like a very long wait.

Maybe she'd peeked out secretly, saw who it was and snuck out the back door.

Or maybe the stout woman had told her what I'd done and they were in the back room snickering.

I could feel myself blushing again.

Then the door opened up.

And there she stood.

She looked a little worn out, actually. Her beautiful mahogany-colored hair was tied back in a bun that was starting to come apart. The white apron she wore over her blue gingham dress was soiled with the colors of four or five different medicines. And there was just a hint of sweat across her brow. She obviously worked hard at the hospital.

"Hello," she said, and blew upward to push hair back from her forehead.

Even slightly exasperated looking, she was beautiful. In a way, she was even *more* beautiful than the other times I'd seen her. Then, she'd been pure princess. But here was her human side, her compassionate side. She was like a beautiful heroine in a book.

"Hello. You look kind of busy."

"There was a bad stagecoach spill," she said, wiping away the sweat on her forehead with the cuff of her dress. "All of a sudden we had seven people to tend to."

"Anybody hurt bad?"

"The driver. Three broken ribs."

I winced at remembered pain. In Yuma, a negro had

broken two of my ribs. Took three, four months for the pain to go away completely. And even all these years later, the ribs would radiate pain every once in a while.

"But look at you," she said. "Your hand."

"Was cutting down a branch with my Bowie knife."

"Let's have a look at it."

"I'd appreciate that."

"I'm glad you asked for me."

Somebody had just handed me the biggest gift I'd ever received. "You are?"

"Yes," she said, leading me into a small white room filled with standing glass cases of medicines and surgical instruments. She took me over to a chair and sat me down.

She went back and closed the door.

"I never really got to say how sorry I was. About the way Cal treated you."

"Oh, that's all right."

"Of course it's not all right. It's terrible. He thinks because my father is a powerful man, he has the right to push anybody around he wants to. It doesn't help that everybody in this part of the Territory is afraid of him. And just for your information, my father doesn't like it any better than I do. He's always arguing with Cal about how he treats people. He's even threatened to disinherit him if he doesn't stop attacking people the way he does."

"I'll bet he wouldn't appreciate that. Being disinherited."

She came over and leaned down close to me. I had a hard time not taking her in my arms.

"Between you and me, I think Cal wishes he'd never had a sister. That way he'd inherit my father's estate all for himself." She straightened up. But still spoke softly. "I'm ashamed to say this but I'm sure there've been times when he's wished something terrible would happen to me. But I shouldn't say that."

"It's all right. You can say anything you want to. I'm your friend."

She stared at me a moment. I wasn't sure why. Maybe she was lonely. She spent a lot of time out at her father's place. She probably didn't know many people her own age. People she could talk to.

"You know, that's how *I* feel, too," she said.

"That we're friends?"

"Exactly."

"Good friends." I had to keep upping the ante. It was like a poker hand you couldn't stop betting.

She laughed. "*Very* good friends." Then, "Now, let's take a look at the wound." She knelt down and undid the bandage.

"That's funny."

"What is?"

"You said you cut yourself up in the hills?"

"Yes."

"This blood looks so fresh."

"It happened right before the wagon was heading back to town. So the cut's still pretty fresh."

She took the blood-soaked cloth off, threw it in a waste can.

"Looks pretty clean. Except for the road dust on the cloth."

"I went down to the creek."

"You did a good job cleaning it out."

I guess I expected her to use regular doctor instruments. Instead, she took out a knitting needle, a straight razor and an embroidery scissors.

"My mother, God love her, taught me this. I'm not really a nurse but I'm pretty good with these things."

"You're so beautiful."

It just came out. Honest to God. I didn't plan it. I didn't think about it. It just came out.

She raised her head. Our eyes met.

"Why, thank you."

"I didn't mean to be forward."

"That wasn't forward at all. That was—nice."

I knew I was blushing.

"The knitting needle I use to look into the wound. Now this'll probably hurt a little."

She parted the lips of the wound expertly with the tip of the knitting needle. She ran it all the way down to the end of the wound, staring down into it as she went.

"It's not that deep," she said.

"Good."

"And it really does look clean."

"Now the razor."

"What's that for?"

"Clean up the edges of the cut where the scabbing has started. I'll clean it all up and then put a little pulverized gunpowder on the edges. That'll make it all nice and antiseptic."

"That's kind of funny."

"What is?"

"That you'd use gunpowder to *help* somebody."

"I said that to myself one day. How odd that is. About gunpowder." She gave me a quick kid grin that nearly knocked me over backwards in my chair. "See, we even *think* alike."

I couldn't believe she was saying these things.

"And now the embroidery scissors."

"You going to make me mittens?"

"No, I'm not going to make you mittens, you dope. I'm going to cut you a length of some nice clean gauze."

"Oh."

"And then you'll be ready to go."

"What if I don't want to go?"

Now it was her turn to blush.

"Don't be funny," she said. But she said it gently.

She finished up in another few minutes.

"How's that?" she said.

"Great. I really appreciate it."

I stood up. She was still crouched down next to my chair.

When she stood up, she swayed. "Gosh, I'm dizzy."

She fell into my arms. I held her. I just prayed I wouldn't get a hard-on.

I'd never held anybody like this. I wanted to tell people. They could have their gold mines. I'd discovered something much better. I could smell her clean hair and clean flesh. I was getting dizzy myself.

I helped her to the chair.

"Oh, thank you."

"My pleasure."

"I guess I was dizzy from being on my haunches so long."

"I'm sure you'll be fine now."

"It's funny."

"What is?"

"Now you're taking care of *me*. It's supposed to be the other way around. I'm the one who works in the hospital."

A knock. Loud. The stout woman peeked in.

"We could really use you in back," she said. "The little girl's worse all of sudden."

"Oh, that sweet little thing," Nora said. "I've been saying prayers for her all afternoon." She nodded to me. "She got thrown from the stagecoach."

Nora stood up. She swayed a little but she stayed on her feet and marched quickly to the doorway.

"I really need to go," she said to me from the doorway. The stout woman had already disappeared, with heavy footsteps down the hall to the back.

"Good luck," I said.

"Say a prayer."

Then, looking worried, she hurried away.

•   •   •

I didn't eat that night, just tumbled into bed and slept.

Or tried to.

Sometime in the middle of the night there was a knock on my door. I was pretty sure I was dreaming it. But when it came again, somebody down the hall shouted, "Shut up! I'm tryin' to sleep!"

Somebody was really at the door.

I crawled through the cloying cobwebs of sleep and turned the doorknob.

"Why don't I buy you a beer?"

"I got to work in the morning," I said.

"So do I."

"It can't wait?"

"It's fresh on my mind."

"Shit."

"C'mon, Sam, don't go gettin' bitchy on me."

He knew I'd say yes if he just stood there long enough, so why even put up an argument?

"I'll be down to the Silver Dollar."

He turned around and walked away. When he got to the door where the yelling had come from, he pounded good and loud. Poor guy was probably so pissed, he wouldn't sleep for a couple of hours.

But if he opened his door, he'd get a surprise he surely didn't want. He'd find out that the guy pounding on it was Earl Cates, the sheriff.

"You seen her lately?" Earl said when I got to the saloon.

"Who?"

"Who? Callie."

"Oh, no, I haven't."

"What happened to your job out to the mansion?"

I told him about my scrape with Cal.

"He's a mean son of a bitch."

"Yeah," I said. "I noticed."

"And he hates his sister."

"God, how could you hate Nora?"

He didn't say anything. Just watched me. And then he laughed out loud. "Oh, Sam, you dope!"

The saloon was crowded, noisy. Nobody heard him insult me.

"What?"

"You done it again, didn't you?"

"Done what?"

"Fell in love."

"What makes you think that?"

"The way you say her name, you dumb shit. You should hear yourself. All sappy'n shit. Lord. You done it again."

"I wish you'd stop sayin' that, Earl."

"It was bad enough with Callie. No matter what she did to you, you couldn't ever let go. She was out of your league in one direction—and Nora is sure as hell out of your league in the other direction. Callie's too smart for you and Nora's this timid little sheltered thing who lives in a castle."

"She's a nice girl."

"You damn bet she's nice. You know where she spent six years?"

"Where?"

"Convent school."

"With nuns?"

"Damned right with nuns. And her old man ain't even a fish-eater. But he figured it'd be a good place for Nora to get all refined and the like. They taught her all that fancy bullshit. How to dress like a lady. How to walk like a lady. How to listen to fancy music." He shook his head. "Son, you got to find yourself a nice, decent town girl somewhere and get yourself a good, steady job and raise yourself a family."

Nice, decent town girl. Good, steady job. Raise a family.

Coming from the Earl Cates I'd been in prison with, this was pretty hard to accept. Sometimes I still had my suspicions about Earl. That his religion was all a ruse. That he hid the real Earl inside of it.

"Don't believe it, do you?"

"No."

He smiled. "I had me a heart attack, son."

"You did?"

"Four years ago. Right after we got out of Yuma. Best thing that ever happened to me."

"It was?"

"It sure was. And you know why? It changed me. They thought I was gonna die. They had me in a hospital bed for a week. And all the time I laid there, I thought of every rotten thing I'd done in my life. And I made myself sick. Physically sick. And I knew I didn't want to be like that no more. *Couldn't* be like that. Because when you have a heart attack, you learn how weak human beings really are. And that's what I'd spent my whole life doing—taking advantage of people weaker than me. So I changed. If you want to call it God, that's fine. I just call it changing. I wanted to do something right with my life for a change. So when this job came open, I rode up here and told the town council the truth about my background. And about my heart attack. And how it changed me. Not all of them bought it. There's six members on the town council and two of them are still waiting for me to start running liquor and whores. But the others gave me a chance. And I want to do right by them."

And I believed him. Or most of me did, anyway. This wasn't the kind of thing Earl would joke about.

"I'm worried about Ham."

"How so?" I said.

"Callie."

"Oh. Yeah."

"You know about them, then."

"Callie told me he's in love with her."

He drank some of his beer. "Sometimes, I wish he was a flower the way other people do. He wouldn't get in so much trouble. He's got the same problem you do. He always goes after impossible women."

"Callie feels sorry for him."

"Yeah, but she also keeps him danglin' on her string, don't think so she don't."

"Why would she do that?"

"Because she needs him for something. And that's what I wanted to talk to you about."

"If something's up, Earl, I don't know about it."

"She didn't say anything to you about having any plan or anything?"

"Nope."

"You know how Callie is. She ain't happy unless she's got herself involved in something dangerous."

And that was true. She was attracted to anything forbidden. The fastest way to get Callie to do something was to tell her it was risky.

"Well, there's one thing kind've funny, I guess."

"What's that?"

I told him about Ham watching Nora and writing things down in his notebook.

"Damn," he said.

"What?"

"I don't want to say anything till I talk to Ham."

He put his beer glass down, empty. "I appreciate your help."

"I didn't think I helped you."

"Oh, you helped me, all right." He smiled sadly. "Unfortunately."

He clapped me on the back and walked out between the batwings. He looked to be in some kind of hurry.

I was late getting to work. It was a day when all my newly bruised muscles announced themselves to my sleep-deprived body. I thought I'd gotten into the rhythm of it but I learned otherwise. I had several days to go before I could do this without pain.

I ate a big dinner that night. They put me in the back of the café. It was a large place with Rochester lamps. Everything was clean. And it didn't smell meaty, either. Lot of places smelled like slaughterhouses.

I was just starting to eat when they came in, Nora and her father and her brother Cal. They weren't dressed fancy but they were dressed well. She wore a tan jacket, white blouse and a pleated riding skirt. The candlelight made Nora's face look even more beautiful. Especially her dark eyes and her innocent mouth.

She didn't see me but Cal did. And as soon as he did, he excused himself from the table and started back toward me.

I was scared and angry at the same time. No way did I want to look bad in front of Nora or her father. If he started a fight, I'd have no choice but to throw some punches myself. But that would be the end of it as far as Nora went.

She looked back now. She looked scared, too.

Cal turned to the left before he got to my table. He went over to the man in the vest with the handlebar mustache. He was the owner. They both looked back at me. Cal whispered something to him and smirked. The man nodded.

Cal went back to his table. He didn't look at me.

I could see Cal and Nora arguing.

I wondered what he'd said to the owner.

I didn't have to wait long to find out.

"I'm sorry, sir," the owner said. He was fifty, chunky, and he looked uneasy. "But we've got such a crowd waiting to be seated, I'll have to ask you to leave. You've been here quite a while."

"I just started eating."

"I'm sorry. It's just, well, you're not a regular. And we've got to think of our regulars first."

"And this wouldn't have anything to do with what Cal just said to you?"

"No, sir. Not at all."

He was a pretty good liar. Smooth.

"And if I don't leave?"

"I'm not going to charge you anything, sir. There's no reason for a ruckus."

"You do this all the time? Make room for the regulars?"

"All the time."

He was good, all right.

I didn't want a ruckus and he seemed to sense that.

I looked down the long room at Cal. He was watching with amused interest. His father was patting Nora's hand. She looked angry and upset.

I stood up.

"I appreciate this, sir."

"I'll bet you do. Otherwise you'd have Cal on your ass."

I thought of brushing past their table but decided against it. I didn't want to upset Nora any more. I wanted to show her father I was a reasonable type. Not a hothead like his son.

There was a back door and I took it.

The railroad tracks in back shone with moonsilver. I followed them for a long time. I felt like shit. The frogs and the owls and the distant train cries made me feel better. All I could think of was Nora.

I finally turned back toward town.

I went to a saloon and had enough beer to make me sleepy. I slept pretty good that night.

But when I woke up there was this *absence* in me. The absence was Nora. This was a lot worse than Callie. This was a lot worse than anybody.

The day was late September hot. I puked a couple of times at work. I wasn't sure why. Maybe it was Nora. Probably it was Nora.

When I got back to my room that night, Earl was waiting for me.

"You look bad, son."

"Tired."

"It's that gal. You're just making yourself miserable. She's just plain out of your reach."

I went over and started to wash some of the day off in the bowl. "How come you're here?"

"I want you to do me a favor."

I dried off. "Like what?"

"Get Ham drunk. He's as bad at drinking as you are. It won't take much."

"You still haven't found out what's going on?"

"Suspicions. Nothing else. Not yet. That's where you come in."

"Maybe he won't talk."

"Maybe. But it's worth a try. I don't want to see him get in no trouble. He's had a sad life. He's all caught up in Callie now and the good Lord only knows what she's got in mind for him."

"Why not just ask Callie?"

"Now, there's a hot one. You think Callie'd ever tell me the truth?"

"Sometimes she tells the truth."

"Sometimes. Not very often."

I threw the towel on the bureau. Went over and sat down on a chair. "Where's he drink?"

"Usually the Golden Rail."

"What time?"

"After supper. Usually about now."

"It makes me feel funny, Earl."

"I know it does, son. But it needs to be done. We're trying to help him is what we're trying to do."

I sighed. "Well, I'll need a little food first."

"Stop by one of our fine cafés and then just wander on over to the Golden Rail."

"Maybe he's with Callie."

"Nope. Callie's got herself a new beau."

"You serious?" It was funny. I thought it was all dead in me for Callie but I felt an odd little quirk of jealousy when he said that.

"Deputy's seen her down in that river pavilion every night for four nights running. Same man."

"Any idea who it is?"

"Nope. They haven't gotten close enough to get a

good look at him. They only recognized *her* because of the red hair. So you don't have to worry about Ham bein' with her."

"Wonder if Ham knows."

"He's known about the rest of them."

"And he didn't walk away?"

"You never walked away, son. And she cheated on you for years."

"Yeah, I guess that's right, isn't it?" I felt all churned up inside.

"Well, you learn anything, stop by my house later tonight."

"You won't be asleep?"

"I might be asleep. But I'll wake up for you. And Ham."

I put on a clean shirt and walked out of the hotel with him.

Chapter 7

I didn't have any trouble finding him.

He stood at the far end of the bar by himself, sipping beer from a glass. He had his derby pushed back on his head and he looked unhappy. Seeing me didn't seem to make him any happier. "I'm not in the mood for talking, Conagher." His voice startled me at first, the way it always did.

"Who said I wanted to talk?"

"You got an answer for everything, don't you?"

I laughed. "Don't I wish." I wanted to try and match his mood. Maybe he'd feel more disposed toward talking.

I ordered a beer and drank half of it in silence.

He sighed a lot. And worked his jaw muscles. He'd look mad and then he'd look sad and then he wouldn't

look nothing at all. Like he was just dead or something. Woman trouble.

"How's it going out to the mansion?"

"Thought you weren't going to talk."

"I just asked a fucking civil question."

He stared at me. "It's goin' all right, I guess."

He went back to staring at his beer.

I decided he wasn't going to talk. I started toward a
table. Might as well sit down and enjoy the beer.

Behind me, he said, "Mind if I join you?"

"Free world."

He joined me. The saloon had a good-sized crowd.
It was the right time of night. They kept the player
piano low enough so you could talk. The loudest noise
was a table filled with poker players. They kept arguing with each other. The rest of the men just wanted to
get drunk.

"I'm havin' trouble with her again, Sam."

"Well, I coulda told you that. Hell, I *did* tell you
that."

"Serious trouble. Man trouble."

"Hell, Ham, it ain't serious. They come and go with
her. They don't mean anything in particular."

"You ever get used to it?"

"No."

"She says it ain't none of my business. That I don't
got no hold on her."

"She's probably right, Ham. You don't even go out
with her."

"Yeah, but I love her and she knows that."

I thought of what Earl had said. About her meeting somebody down by the river every night. Sneaking around like that meant one thing: whoever he was, he was married.

"Any idea who he is?"

"Nope."

"You could follow her."

"Yeah, and if I seen him kiss her, I'd go wild. I'd kill him with my hands, Sam, and then where would I be?"

We drank some. Looked around.

"Earl said he hasn't seen you much."

"Been busy."

"With what?"

Ham looked at me a moment and then smiled. "Earl sent you, didn't he?"

"Sent me?"

"That son of a bitch. He's checking up on me, wants to save my soul. He wants me to get rid of Callie, for a start."

"That'd be a pretty good start."

"Tell him it's none of his business what I'm up to."

I said, "Every time I see you around Nora, I see you writing in your little notebook. Makes me curious."

"You nosy bastard."

"The way I figure it, you're writing down the times she does certain things."

"That's the way you figure it, huh?"

"I mean, if I was going to kidnap somebody, that's exactly how I'd start out. I'd write down what they do every day. Figure out the best time and the best place to nab them."

I couldn't read him any better than I ever could. But he gave a slight start when I mentioned the word "kidnap." And I saw his right hand grip his glass handle harder.

"She'd be worth a lot of money."

"You're wrong, Sam."

"This sounds like something Callie'd come up with. It's got everything—danger, money and a chance to rub some rich people's faces in the dirt."

"Rich people ought to treat Callie a lot better than they have in her life. She's as good as they are."

"She's going to get you hanged, Ham."

"Maybe she's smarter than you think. Maybe *I'm* smarter than you think."

"Nothing to do with smart, Ham. Has to do with power. Man like her father, he'd never rest until you were dead."

"Fella could be in Mexico by then. Or Europe. Living the high life."

"With Callie right by his side, I bet."

He blushed. "That'd be my business."

I sat back. Rolled a cigarette. Smoked it for a time. "Ham."

"I don't want no more lectures. I'm sick of fucking lectures all my life."

"I just want you to consider something."

"What?"

"What if, say, this kidnapping comes off?"

"I told you, there ain't no kidnapping."

"Let's just pretend there is. For the sake of conversation, Ham. We're sitting here, we might as well talk about something."

"Then let's talk about baseball."

"Let's finish the other conversation first."

He frowned. "I got to go, anyway."

"Just a couple more minutes." Before he could protest, I said, "So, say the kidnapping comes off and the girl—let's call her Nora—this Nora is returned home safely to her father. Your problem is over, right?"

"I guess."

"But it isn't. Because you're dealing with a woman who won't even go out with you." I decided to let him have it. It was the only way. "Who makes fun of you behind your back because your voice is so high-pitched."

The rage came fast to his eyes. "I could kill you right here, Sam. You better watch your mouth."

"You think this is the kind of woman who's going to keep her word and split the kidnap money with you?"

"You son of a bitch."

He lunged for me. I sat back.

The bartender said, "Hey, you two, you break anything, you pay for it."

"Cool down, Ham. I'm trying to help you."

"You're jealous."

"I am?"

"Damn right you are. Because she's all done with you. At least I've got a chance with her," Ham said.

"You do?"

"She told me that. She said she needs a little time is all. To kinda get used to me."

He made me want to cry. For him.

"Ham, listen—"

He got up. "Don't never cut her down in front of me anymore, Sam. That's fair warning."

"I'm tryin' to help you is all, Ham."

"I don't need you *or* your help. You understand, Sam?"

He jabbed a thick finger at me then stalked across the open area between the bar and the batwings.

I sat there for another beer. It was a kidnapping, all right, what was being planned. No doubt about that now.

I had to stop it for Nora's sake.

Callie and Ham were in on it. I wondered about Callie's new lover. Maybe he was in on it, too. I needed to find out who he was. I checked my railroad watch. It'd be worth swinging down by the river again tonight, find out who she was seeing. So I could tell Earl everything.

The small town park was all deep blue shadow and silence except for a few night birds. When you walked down the center of it, you couldn't even hear the river. There was a tiny band box and a statue of the town founder. The park was a block long by half-a-block wide. To get to the river you had to take one of two paths. There was a wall of bramble keeping you from any other course.

I walked that wall, listening carefully for any sound. There were nooks of shadow along the river where lovers could hide and be left alone, especially at this time of night. But nothing; no sound.

I eased on down to the water's edge. The river ran silver in the moonlight. You could smell wet earth and new grass. I wondered if they were behind me, in the nook of trees or shrubs, watching me and laughing at me.

I walked the length of the park and found nothing. Far down in the water I saw a fisherman throwing his line out from a rowboat. He looked noble and lonely silhouetted against the sky that way.

I tried the river pavilion. You could almost smell the meals that had been cooked here on summer holidays, hear the kids, and the snappy band. But now the pavilion was empty.

Across the street from the western end of the park were two small barns. The town kept its maintenance equipment in one and its horses in the other.

I looked around. If Callie and her friend were anywhere around here, they had to be in one of those barns, and it was most likely the one with the equipment. The sweet scent of horse shit is a little *too* sweet for romance.

The barn was dark. The front doors were padlocked. I went around to the side and peeked in a dusty window. Water wagon for dusty streets; shovels and rakes and twenty-five pound bags of lime; roofing materials and window frames and new board for sidewalks. But nothing moving.

And then a voice.

I stayed as still as possible. Listened.

Had I imagined it? Seemed so because now I couldn't hear it.

I was just turning to go when I heard it again.

From inside. Callie's voice.

I walked over to the side door. This one was padlocked, too.

I went all the way around the barn to the other side door. Padlocked. Or so I thought till I looked closely. It was actually hanging open. But you had to look hard to see it. Somehow Callie had managed to get a key. All she would have to do is be nice to the man who worked here and he'd probably help her out. Callie was good at things like that.

I gently took the lock off. Put my ear to the door.

She was talking again. But in a much lower voice this time.

They could be in there a long time.

There was only one open door and I was standing in it with my gun drawn. I was about to find out who Callie's friend was.

"C'mon out, Callie. You and your friend."

Nothing. Then frantic whispers coming from the far side of the barn and to the right. And up. They were in the loft.

"C'mon out, Callie."

"What're you doing here, Sam?"

"I want to talk to you."

"You don't have any right to do this."

"Well, ever since I found out what you and Ham are up to, I figure I *do* have a right."

"That bastard—"

"He didn't tell me anything, Callie. I put it together myself."

"I'll make sure you get a gold star for the day."

"You and your friend get down here right now."

"I'm here alone."

"Sure you are."

"I am."

"Just get down here. Now. Both of you."

"You're going to be very disappointed when you find out it's just me," she said.

That was when I got knocked out.

Later on, I could picture it easy enough. While Callie and I talked, her friend found something to throw at me. If he fired a gun, that might bring people running. But if he just hit me with something, he could get away with no problem.

When I came to several minutes later, I found what he'd hit me with. A nice fist-sized chunk of red brick. It was up to the job.

Blood had dampened the right side of my head. The brick had left a knot.

I sat up slowly. My head was aggrieved with pain. My vision was foggy.

From the darkness in front of me, a voice said, "You had it coming, Sam. What I do is none of your damned business."

"See you're still hanging around with nice guys."

"He could have shot you instead of using a rock."

She stepped into the moonlight angling through the open door.

"Get up. We've got to get out of here. I promised the guy who gave me the key I'd have it back by ten."

"I figured it was something like that."

I took a long time getting to my feet and nearly fell facedown in doing so. She didn't help at all.

I got up and wobbled over to the door. Leaned against the frame. She started to push me out of the way so she could close the door and lock up.

I gripped her wrist.

"I know what you're up to."

"Good for you."

"Ham writing down what Nora does during the day."

"I should've known a genius like you would figure it out."

"Earl's on to you, too."

"Now I'm *really* scared."

"You don't want to cross Earl, believe me."

"I know. He's a righteous man."

She ripped her wrist free.

"You may think you know what's going on, Sam. But you don't. And you never did. You think because you read all those books, you're smart. But you're not.

You live in your little make-believe world, Sam. White knights and princesses and dragons. All those stupid Grimm Brothers stories you used to read me. That's the world you live in, Sam. I just wish you knew how much people laughed at you behind your back. All high and mighty with your books. Just the way Earl is all high and mighty with his religion. Now, get out of the way so I can lock this door."

She locked up and walked away.

I tried to catch up to her but I couldn't. Too dizzy. Too much pain. I was going to be in fine shape for work tomorrow.

When I finally got going, I hobbled on over to a doc's place and had him fix me up. Everything he did hurt like hell.

Then I went back to my room and washed up and lay down. It didn't take me long to fall asleep.

I had a funny dream. I was this white knight and behind me a whole town full of Callies were laughing at me good and loud.

Then Nora appeared in a castle window and begged me to save her from her prison. I was just about to when the dawn dogs started yapping and the new day was here.

Chapter 8

I guess it was while I was shaving that I got the idea. I didn't have any real evidence yet that Callie and Ham were going to kidnap Nora. Suspicions but nothing more. I wouldn't have any *real* evidence until they'd actually taken her. And by then it'd be too late.

Unless I got ready now.

If I quit my job and spent the next few days secretly following Callie and Ham around, they just might lead me to the place where they planned to hide Nora.

Then I'd be a hero for sure in Nora's eyes.

She'd be a prisoner and I'd come in and rescue her.

Even her father would have to look at me differently. Maybe even Cal himself would begrudgingly come to like me.

I finished shaving and went to the café for breakfast.

I kept going back and forth on my new idea. One minute it seemed like genius, the next it seemed to have too many things wrong with it.

What if there was a shoot-out in the hiding place and Nora got killed in the cross fire?

What if they changed hiding places at the last minute?

What if they backed out of the kidnapping altogether? Wouldn't it be better to at least warn John Rutledge that somebody was planning to kidnap his daughter? I wouldn't be as much of a hero, but he'd sure as hell be appreciative, especially with Earl backing up my story. I'd go to work and it'd be just like any other day.

But it was funny, soon as I got to the company dock where the wagon waited to take us to the timber, I said to the driver, "Tell Jennings I'm quitting."

"Shit, man, you're makin' good money."

"I know. But somethin's come up."

"A gal, probably." He grinned and spat an arc of tobacco juice over my shoulder.

"Climbin' into the right little gal is like climbin' into a nice warm bed you never wanna get out of."

I grinned, letting him have his story. "You got that right. And tell Jennings I appreciated the work."

The next thing I did was find the wagon that took Ham and Callie out to the Rutledge mansion. They might have a short day. The sky was overcast. Rain clouds rolled in from the east. It was cold, too.

• • •

It didn't rain that day.

Or the next.

Ham and Callie went to work every day and got back just before suppertime. Ham stuck mostly to the saloons. Callie surprised me by staying in her hotel room. What had happened to the party girl?

It took me two nights to figure it out.

I stood in the alley behind Callie's hotel. I wanted to watch and make sure she didn't sneak out the back door.

It was noisy, all the saloons; and smelly, the cafés filling their garbage cans, and all the dogs and cats and rats and coons of various kinds gorging themselves.

He was a smart son of a bitch, I had to give him that.

He didn't go in the front entrance of the hotel. He didn't even go in the back entrance.

He jumped from the roof of the adjacent building to the roof of the hotel then swung down to the top floor of the fire escape and let himself in the door. She was staying on that floor, right next to the fire escape. I'd checked.

Nobody was likely to see him this way. And anybody who was watching for Callie would think she was just staying in for the evening.

I couldn't get a good look at him while he was flying through the air. He wore a sloppy black hat with a wide brim that kept his face in shadow. He also wore a black duster that kept his body covered.

Maybe I didn't know *who* he was but I sure as hell knew *what* he was.

Kidnapping somebody as important as Nora, Callie sure as hell wouldn't trust Ham alone. She'd bring somebody else in. Somebody smart.

I went in the front entrance of the hotel.

The clerk was busy with a couple of drummers and didn't even look my way.

I'd thought about going up the fire escape but Callie and her friend might hear me.

I climbed the stairs to her floor.

I had a pretty good wait, an hour-and-a-half.

I waited around a corner. Soon as I heard the door open, I'd take a look.

I rolled four smokes. I heard one couple screwing, two drummers rehearsing their sales pitches, one man coughing up enough phlegm to keep me off food for a week, and an old woman sitting in a rocker and singing old Southern songs.

When he came out, he came out fast.

He looked my direction just once and thankfully didn't see me.

It was kind of funny—all his religious bullshit, he'd even managed to fool me, and I knew him just about as well as you can know a guy, being his cell mate.

Callie had gotten herself a smart partner, all right.

And an important one, too—the sheriff of this busy little town, Earl Cates himself.

Part Two

Chapter 9

Seven hours later, Earl Cates sat down next to me at the café counter and said, "I think I'll have *two* breakfasts this morning."

It was a little bit spooky, how he showed up right while I was thinking about him.

What a perfect decoy. The sheriff himself involved in the kidnapping. He could run people around in circles forever. He'd have the money and he'd have Callie.

"Morning," he said to the woman behind the counter. "I'll have two steaks, two orders of fried potatoes and six strips of bacon."

He rolled himself a cigarette while she brought him his coffee.

"You look tired, Sam."

"I was up late."

He smiled. "Not doing anything you're ashamed of, I hope."

"Nope. Just thinking."

He watched me more closely. "You seem a little down at the mouth, too."

"Sun's barely up. You remember how I was."

I almost said "in prison." But that was a phrase that would displease him greatly, undermine his legal authority.

"I had me a *good* night's sleep."

"Good for you."

"Sleep of the innocent," he said.

The woman brought my breakfast.

"I'm so hungry, I feel like stealin' that from you, Sam."

"You bein' the sheriff and all, I wouldn't think you would want to do anything illegal."

"Oh, it crosses your mind, believe me. You've got the gun and you've got the badge and you've got the legal power. And it'd be so easy. You hear about corrupt lawmen all the time."

"You sure do."

"But that's where the good book comes in."

He was going to make me sick with all his good book bullshit. He was going to make me sick and I wouldn't be able to eat my breakfast.

"The Devil, he's a bushwhacker. You know that? He won't come out and fight you clean and fair. You know, man to man. Oh, no. He'll lurk around in the shadows and wait till you're at your weakest point.

And then he'll bushwhack you. And not with bullets, either. Oh, no, the Devil knows there's something a lot deadlier than bullets. And that's temptation. Bullets can kill your body. But what Satan wants is your soul. And that means you need to be mortally wounded by sin—your own sin. So he shoots you with temptation. You understand, son?"

"I sure wish you was a minister," said the enthralled woman as she poured him more coffee. "If you was a minister, every heathen in this here pagan town would come and listen to you, Sheriff. And I swear that's true."

"Well, thank you, Minnie. But vanity is a sin. So any sermonizing I do, well, that credit goes to the Lord. He puts the words in my head. All I do is repeat them."

"See?" she said, astonished. "Just like right now. Just how you made that up right on the spot."

"The Lord made it up right on the spot," Earl reminded her. "The Lord."

It was funny, the only time Earl ever sounded like this—this Bible-thumpin' stuff—was after he'd sinned. It was like he was compensating for what he'd done wrong—and cheated on his wife was what he'd done wrong—by becoming this newspaper cartoon of a Jesus-hollerin' minister.

His food shut him up. He smacked his lips, he rolled his eyes, he patted his belly, he went "ooooh" and he went "ahhhh" and it was embarrassing was what it was, but Minnie kept winking at me and said, "Ain't it cute the way he eats?"

Oh, he was cute all right.

When he started getting filled up, bits of food glistening in his Hickok-style mustache, he leaned a little closer and said, "You find out anything?"

He was trying to learn what I knew. Find out just how dangerous I was. I had no proof. I might take it upon myself to go to Mr. Rutledge, but again, with no proof.

And I wouldn't look like much of a hero, either.

"You know what I was thinkin'?" he said.

"What?"

"Maybe you're wrong about Ham and Callie. Maybe I'm wrong, too."

"Maybe."

"We distrust them based on their past lives. But people could just as easy do the same about us."

I didn't have any choice but to go along.

"Yeah, I suppose you're right."

The idea was to convince me that nothing was going to happen. Then maybe I'd stop bothering Ham and Callie.

"Like I said, I had the same suspicions but when I was praying for Callie and Ham last night, you know what the Lord said to me?"

"I'll bet it was something special."

"Very special, son. And don't think I don't hear the sarcasm in your voice. Very special. He said to me, 'Earl, people give you a chance for a new start when

you come out of prison. You got to do the same for
Callie and Ham. You have to show them the same faith
that people done showed you.'"

I wanted to tell him that it was unlikely that the
Lord, who I sort of believed in down deep, ever used
the phrase "that people done showed you," but why
spoil his roll? He'd be dragging me down to the river
and baptizing me any second now.

"You get my drift, son?"

"I get your drift, Earl."

"We just need to love them and pray for them and
hope that our suspicions ain't true." Then he said, the
first serious thing he'd said all morning, "Just the way
somebody needs to pray for me."

"I guess you're right."

He looked startled.

"You do? About Callie and Ham?"

"Yeah."

"I mean, if we had any real proof—"

"Sure, all we've got is Ham following her around
and writing down all her movements."

"Right," he agreed.

"And Callie all of a sudden coming up with a mysterious lover, who just might be—I mean, if you was
cynical and didn't show people the same faith that
people done showed you and me—you might think he
was maybe helping her out with the kidnapping, which
is why he didn't want to be identified."

"Exactly."

"And just because Ham practically admitted to me

that that's what they were up to—" I shook my head. "Cynicism is another weapon the Devil uses, I guess."

"I guess I don't know that word."

"Cynicism?"

"Yeah. Though I'd like to. The Lord is always after me to improve my vocab—" He stopped. "How do you say that word?"

"Vocabulary."

"Right." He nodded his head. "He's always after me to improve my vocabulary."

"Cynicism means you don't give people the benefit of the doubt."

"Oh."

He still didn't get it.

"That you tend to distrust people and think the worst of them."

I could see recognition in his eyes. "The way you and me see Callie and Ham."

"Exactly."

"Cynicism. That's a word that you're going to hear me using a lot. That is one fine word."

He looked up at the tocking clock on the wall and said, "Well, time for me to push off. Check the prisoners, get the day going." He clapped me on the back. "You're gonna be a believer one of these days, son. You mark my words."

Minnie watched him all the way out the door. Jesus and all the apostles couldn't have inspired her with any more awe.

• • •

On Saturday, they led me into the mountains.

They left mid morning. It was another overcast day, rain clouds in the west making the snow on the mountains seem almost as dingy as the clouds themselves.

Callie and Ham.

Callie had never been much for horses and she showed it that day. She was always whacking the animal to hurry up, to slow down, to angle this way or that. She was also good at screaming at it. I stayed half a mile behind, but even so I could hear her screeching at the horse.

Ham knew horses. Even on a couple of narrow mountain passes, he guided his horse with assurance and skill.

A couple of times, Callie damned near went down into the river far below. It might well have been intentional on the horse's part. Sure, he'd be dead but *she'd* be dead, too. And that couldn't be all bad, now could it?

When they reached the mesa, I tied my horse to a jack pine, grabbed my binoculars and went to have a look-see.

The cabin had once been some kind of line shack, most likely used by the mine companies. It was up behind a small forest of pines, and had disintegrated pretty bad under the rains and the snows of the Territory.

They ground-tied their mounts and went inside. They stayed in there for twenty minutes or so.

I wondered where they'd grab her and how they'd

subdue her. That's where a lot of kidnappings went
bad. In the east there'd been a coal baron's kid whose
head had been accidentally slammed into the edge of a
building by one of the kidnappers. The kid died about
twelve hours later. A mob took care of the two kidnappers.

I was especially worried about how Callie would
treat her, given Callie's feelings toward anybody who
seemed even slightly rich or educated or refined. This
would give her a perfect opportunity to take some of
her resentments out.

Ham, on the other hand, would do whatever Callie
told him.

When they came out, they walked to the edge of the
forest and started scanning the area surrounding the
mesa. This was probably the best hideout they could
find, though it wasn't exactly ideal. Depending on
how many posse members John Rutledge came up
with, they wouldn't be safe in this cabin for more than
two days at most.

They had one thing in their favor.

The sheriff, who would no doubt be leading the
posse, would be doing all he could to confuse everybody.

He'd be sure to advise Rutledge to pay the ransom
money immediately.

He'd also be sure to tell him all sorts of horror stories about other kidnappings that had ended up with
sons and daughters dead.

So, right now they were looking to see which path the posse was likely to take.

You didn't see the cabin unless you knew it was there. But somebody in town was sure to know about it.

They did have the advantage of escaping up the mountain through the forest. If the posse started to close in, Callie and Ham could drag Nora out the back way and have a damned good chance of eluding the mob.

And, once again, Earl would be there to delay them every way he could.

It was dark when we got back to town. Callie and Ham split up.

I went to my room and lay down.

I had a dream about Nora. They kidnapped her and she broke away from them and ran to a black lake and the lake was filled with snakes and the snakes dragged her down and she disappeared. I waited by the lake until long after midnight, when the snakes began to hiss as they dragged her body ashore and dumped it on the silver sands. And there were no trees, no rocks, no grass, no life of any kind, and the lake was only a sandy bed now, and even the snakes vanished, and the moon turned bloodred and when I looked down at her she began to crack and crumble like an ancient statue, and blood began to pour from her and sink into the sand until I was standing on a lake of her boiling red blood, and the moon turned the color of a lemon, and then the snows came and tore the clothes from me and I stood naked in a lashing blizzard.

And then I woke up.

I sat up on my bed and rolled a cigarette.

I couldn't escape the dream.

Not the images of it. Those were gone. But the *feeling* of it. That's what I couldn't escape.

I was restless.

I drank some whiskey, I masturbated, I lay on my bed and said prayers.

Was I doing it the right way? Shouldn't I maybe go to Mr. Rutledge now and tell him what I knew? What if I rescued her and they still didn't regard me as anything more than scum? That would be the worst joke of all. If I rescued her and she still didn't want anything to do with me.

Chapter 10

The next day, the banners went up for the fire department contest a week from today. They were red, white and blue banners that stretched across the main street. They looked smart and citified and people would stand in the dirt street with their hands shielding their eyes from the sun and gawk at them. Just stand there and gawk a long, long time as if this was some new modern invention, these banners, and by God they were just flat out enthralled.

I did some gawking myself but mostly I sat in the little park, in the good nourishing sunlight, and read my *Tom Sawyer*. Every once in a while somebody would stop by and say, "Ain't that a book for little kids?" Acting smart and all. I'd just smile and let them have their fun.

I was reading along when Callie appeared in front

of me. She looked especially pretty in her dangerous way.

"Pigeon shit," she said.

"What?"

"Pigeon shit on my side of the bench."

"Oh."

"Hand me a page of that newspaper you're sitting on."

"Then I'll get pigeon shit on me."

"There're two or three pages there. I just want one."

So I did the chivalrous thing and got up and gave her one sheet of the newspaper and then sat my ass back down on the bench.

I went back to my reading.

"Don't you ever get sick of it?"

"Sick of what?"

"Reading."

"Not very often. You ever get sick of it?"

"What?"

"Being a fallen woman."

"Don't start your bullshit, Sam."

"I talked to Ham the other day."

"He told me. That kidnapping thing you came up with is crazy."

"Sure it is."

"I know you don't approve of me any more since you got book-smart in prison." She laughed. "You get book-smart and Earl gets God-smart. What a pair you are."

I liked her again for just a few seconds there. I could

smell her again and feel her again and taste her again
but it wasn't just the sex. It was the sweetness she
sometimes showed. A person rough as her, when she's
sweet it can break your heart sometimes. There's an
innocence about it because it's so rare. I thought of
how hard her life had been and how she'd never had
much chance of becoming anything but a whore, not
with her ambitious side. And so I reached over and
took her hand and just held it. I didn't even give a
damn that she was in cahoots with Earl and was going
to kidnap Nora and was probably going to kill Ham
after it was all over.

For just that brief time, there in the breeze and the
sunshine and the birdsong and the clock above the
bank doors tolling noon . . . for just that moment I
didn't hate either of us the way I usually did . . . or
blame each of us the way I usually did . . . there was
a sweetness in *both* of us for just that moment and
she must have felt it, too, because she took my hand
and put it to her lips and kissed it gently and then
held it to her cheek and said, "It just gets so messed
up, Sam."

"Yeah, I know."

"I wish I wasn't such a whore. I'm sorry for the way
I treated you."

"I wasn't any prize."

"You never beat me."

I smiled. "That's because you scared me. You've
got a hell of a punch."

And then all of a sudden in that silence it got a little

awkward again and I could see she felt tense around me the way I felt around her because we both knew what was going to happen. She was going to kidnap Nora.

She said, "How's your head?"

"From the rock your friend threw?"

"Uh-huh."

"I survived."

"Yeah. I can see that. But it might still hurt."

"It's all right."

A silence again.

"I really did love you once, Sam."

"I know."

"And I really did try."

"I know."

"Deep down in my soul I'm not a whore."

"If you say so." I got a mean edge again, thinking of all the times she'd cheated on me.

"You won't even give me that, huh?"

"If you say deep down in your soul you're not a whore, then I accept that."

"Is that the same as believing it?"

"Sort of."

She looked at me. "I guess I don't blame you."

I lifted up my book.

"I'd really like to get some reading done."

"In other words, you want me to go away."

"Yeah."

When she'd first sat down, I figured she wanted information. See if I'd learned any more about the kidnapping, the way Earl had that morning in the café.

But now I saw that she was here for another reason. At least ten times a day, she needed somebody to tell her she was all right. Maybe not a queen. Maybe not a nun. But a decent enough person in a not-so-decent world. She was like a little kid about it, the way she needed those words. I guessed that if she heard them often enough maybe she'd believe them someday herself.

I knew I should have said something nice to her. But I had the edge on. I'd walked in on her screwing some Mex one day and that night things got pretty rough between us and I was crying and shit and just couldn't stop and then when we finally got into bed she told me she was pregnant and she was hurt that I wasn't excited. How could I be excited? Hell, how could I even ever know the kid was mine, the way she slept around? But then it all became moot because a couple of weeks later, in the middle of the night, she was by the window sobbing and I rolled over on to the warm blood of the miscarriage on the sheet.

She stood up.

"You're a fool, Sam. Nora Rutledge. You really think you've got a chance with her?"

"Just get the hell out of here, Callie."

"I see you over here and I come over to try and be nice to you and look at how you treat me."

Then she started crying. And they were real tears.

She always rubbed her wrist scars when she cried for real. Like a bad luck talisman or something.

But I still couldn't say anything good to her because now my head was filled with the Mex and all the other bastards she'd cheated with.

She just walked away, and I just let her.

I bought a Winchester that afternoon. I hadn't ever owned one. It felt good in my hand.

I went down by the river and shot at tin cans. I wasn't exactly a marksman. There were some kids and they were laughing about what a bad shot I was sometimes. I laughed along with them.

When I ran out of bullets, I went and sat on the grass across from where I'd caught Callie and her friend in the barn. I thought of what a strange old world it was. I got that from reading, too. How writers can't really ever explain things, either, all the strange twists and turns life takes. They can describe it and they can make you feel it but they sure can't explain it.

I'd loved Callie so long and now I didn't love her anymore. I loved Nora even though I didn't know her at all.

I just sat there and watched the sunlight play through the trees, the shadow-jump and shadow-sway of the summer leaves on the summer river, and it was so beautiful and timeless. A million years ago somebody just like me had probably sat next to a river like this and thought the same thoughts and come to the same conclusions; that you can describe your feelings and you can feel your feelings but you can't explain them. Like how watching that play of shadow on water makes you sad sometimes, that maybe only God can explain those feelings if He actually exists. How that shadow-jump and shadow-play can make you sad, the way a woman can make you sad, can make you want to cry sometimes and you don't even know why, and it doesn't make any difference if you're rich or poor, or nigger or white or injun. You've got these same sad feelings that sometimes just don't make any sense at all, and there's no use talking about them because you'd just sound foolish or stupid. The way your friend would sound foolish or stupid if he tried to explain them to you.

I did the only thing I could. I went and got myself some drinks.

He was riding down the street on a big chestnut when I saw him, imposing as ever. Should have been a judge, that Roman-senator face and white hair, three-piece suit, expensive boots, a Colt strapped to his hip and a rifle jammed into the saddle scabbard. John Rutledge.

I stood on the sidewalk. Watched him dismount. Watched him walk into the bank. Watched the way a working man nervously held the door for him when he recognized who was coming his way. Watched the too-friendly way Rutledge thanked the man, the way a politician does, all big and hollow, wanting to show the workingman that Rutledge was just like him after all.

I went over to his horse. I couldn't tell you why exactly. I guess somehow it brought me closer to Nora. The animal and the gear belonged to the Rutledge family. As did Nora herself.

I patted the horse and touched the saddle.

I wondered if Nora had ever ridden this particular horse.

Probably not. She had her own.

Maybe this was the kind of imposing animal they'd give me when I became part of the family. Their way of telling me that not only had I saved their daughter, I had become a key member of the clan. I'd have a city job and I'd wear three-piece suits and I'd have my picture taken holding my derby so formally, the way they do in those Eastern pictures, and each year for five, six years the pictures would be different because there'd be a new little one who had to be included. They'd look like their mother, even the boys, so handsome and fine, like something expensive and valuable that gets passed down from generation to generation, and is kept under key so that it doesn't get ruined by common fingers touching it too much.

"If you don't move away from my animal, sir, I will shoot you on this very spot."

His voice suited his noble Roman head.

Before I had turned completely to face him, he pushed the barrel of his Colt in my face.

"Exactly, sir, what are you doing?"

"I . . ."

I was frozen in place. Speechless.

"You'll explain to me, or by God I'll see that you explain to the sheriff."

People were starting to encircle us.

Not every day that John Rutledge pulls a gun on somebody.

I said, "I was just—admiring—your horse and saddle, Mr. Rutledge."

"Not about to steal my rifle?"

"No, sir." I managed to hold up my Winchester. "I just bought my own this afternoon."

"That was a very foolish thing to do," he said, "and a damned good way to get yourself shot."

That was twice, in a very short time, that I'd been called foolish today.

He took my Winchester. Examined it.

"This is actually a better piece than mine."

"Thank you, sir."

He was aware of the crowd.

When a man rules a town the way Rutledge did, he can run it two ways. He can be a tyrant. Or he can be a benevolent despot. The trick with the despot is to appear *not* to be a despot.

He decided to amuse his growing audience.

"If anything," he said, his blue eyes gleaming with humor, looking around at the crowd, "I'm the one who should be robbing *you.*"

They knew enough to laugh. And loudly.

He handed me back my Winchester.

"You look familiar to me." And then he snapped his fingers. "The other night in the café."

"Yessir."

"You had some sort of dust-up with my son Cal."

"Yessir."

"And he got you kicked out."

"Yessir."

"Just so you know—in case you haven't already figured it out for yourself—Cal's a hothead. Not a bad young man. But a hothead. I'm afraid I spoiled him after his mother died. I tried to spoil my daughter but she wouldn't let me. She's too sensible a girl. Anyway, getting you run out of there was all Cal's idea. My daughter was embarrassed about it and I was damned mad. Nora told me about the run-in you and Cal had out at the house. He was just throwing his weight around was all. I'm sorry."

Once again, I was speechless for a moment.

"Oh, it wasn't much. I just went somewhere else and ate."

He eased me gently aside, raised his boot to fit it into the stirrup and then heaved himself up into his saddle.

"I'm sorry I was sharp with you there. I just didn't know what you were up to is all."

I blurted, "Please tell Nora I said hello."

He looked at me hard. "If you mean *Miss* Nora, I'll be glad to pass the message along."

"Yessir," I said. "That's exactly what I meant. *Miss* Nora."

He smiled, satisfied, doffed his white Stetson to the ladies in the crowd and rode off.

Chapter 11

I was having a beer when Earl showed up. He walked around the saloon, enjoying all the deference and fear, and then came over to me.

"How's the beer today?"

"Good."

"Wish I could have one." You can see that in alkies sometimes. How they'll talk about it for a while before they actually do it. He was the kind of alkie who could stay dry for long periods of time and then he'd go on a tear. Maybe outlaw sex was that way for him, too.

"You're s'posed to be dry, Earl."

"A couple of beers and a good meal. Now, that to me is a good evening. You like home cooking?"

"Sure. Who doesn't?"

"Believe it or not, I know folks who like cafés better. But that's why the good Lord give a man a wife, the way I figure it. To put a good meal on the table."

I remembered my own ma.

"And to cook and clean and wash and nurse and worry." She died at thirty-four, a sweet-faced woman with a sadness I don't think even my father understood. She stood at the only window a lot, staring out on the prairie. I always wondered what she was looking for. Dawn to midnight she worked. The old man worked hard, too, but at least he got to sleep at a decent hour. When she died, and the local doc couldn't explain it, her sister said, "She died of bein' plumb wore out." And that was as good an explanation as any.

"You like roast beef?"

I smiled. "No, Earl. I hate roast beef."

He smiled back.

"You like potatoes stewed in vegetables?"

"No, Earl, I hate potatoes stewed in vegetables."

His smile got even bigger.

"You like punkin' pie?"

"Now that I hate *especially,* Earl, punkin' pie."

"Well, consider yourself invited."

"To where?"

"To my house. For supper tomorrow night. You never did meet my wife or my boys."

"Your boys?"

"Well, they're my boys now. Their daddy died when they was young, and Corrina, she never did discipline very good."

"Nice little life, a good woman and two boys."

"The woman's good, and I get down on my knees every day and thank the Lord for her. Like I said, though, the kids, they're another matter."

"Oh?"

"Don't obey me worth a darn. Wild kids. Used to gettin' their own way all the time." He winked. "Don't want 'em to turn out like you'n me, do we?"

"We sure don't."

"So one understandin' I had with Corrina before the good Lord seen fit to get us hitched, I said, only way I'll be your husband is if you give me the right to straighten out them kids of yours."

"And she has?"

"Yeah, she has. She don't always like it, how I handle a situation I mean, but she don't say nothin'. She just leaves the room and lets me work on the situation."

He drank some of the soda pop that had been set down in front of him a few minutes back.

"She's curious about you," he said.

"Your wife?"

"Uh-huh. That's what she always says, anyway. Why don't you bring Sam around? I'd like to meet him."

"Well, that's nice."

"She's gonna try'n find out all she can."

"About me?"

"Huh-uh. About me. That's why she wants to get you out to the house. Get a couple of beers and a good meal in you and then go to work on you. See if you know any good Earl Cates stories."

"She knows you were in Yuma?"

"Oh, sure. Everybody in these parts does."

"Then what else is there?"

"Well, I never told her much specific. Just said how I'd been a sinner and all and it wasn't worth talkin' about. After she gets the kids to bed, expect her to start askin' you questions about me. I think she's real interested in the women I was with."

"Well, there were a lot of them."

"It's nothin' I'm proud of."

Sure, Earl, I thought. Kidnappings are all right but not running around with women. His Bible-thumping hypocrisy was getting to me. But I wanted to find out what he was up to.

"She know about Callie?"

"Nope," he said.

"Probably best."

"Especially since Callie's right here in town."

He drained his soda. Pushed his glass forward. The bartender was right there.

"Hear you had a little dust-up with Mr. Rutledge."

"Turned out all right."

"You never know which way that boy's gonna go. All depends on his mood. You musta got him in a good one."

"He thought I was trying to steal his rifle. Honest mistake."

"Were you?"

"Hell, no."

"Then why were you at his horse?"

He was playing sheriff, serious sheriff, and it surprised me.

"Just liked the looks of the animal was all."

"Never seen a horse before, huh?"

"That's right, Earl. I never seen a horse before. Why the hell you hard-assin' me?"

"Because he's a citizen I'm sworn to protect."

Protect from kidnappers, too.

"That's awfully fancy talk, Earl."

"I take this job serious, son. I asked the Lord to redeem my life and this is the way He chose to redeem it, and so by gum, I do the best job I can. No slackin'. Even when it involves an old friend."

"You really think I'd be dumb enough to walk up to Rutledge's horse in broad daylight, in the middle of town, with all sorts of people walking by, and try to steal something from his saddle?"

"I was just checkin', Sam. That's all. And you've relieved my mind."

"Well, you haven't relieved mine."

"There's your temper."

"Damn right there's my temper."

The bartender was starting to listen in now. You could tell by the way he angled his head. This was getting good, would make good gossip later tonight, the sheriff hassling his old friend.

"Cool down, son."

"Don't call me, son."

Kidnapping son of a bitch. The hypocrisy was a bone in my throat.

He put a big hand on my shoulder and said, "Right where the creek jags to the east there's a stand of birches, and on the other side of that stand is our place. We'll see you about six."

"Maybe I won't be there."

"Well, I'm gonna tell Corrina you *will* be there, and believe me them Swede women ain't the kind you want to disappoint."

And then it left me, that pure rage. It was like some kind of intoxicant. It was what had gotten me into so much trouble when I was young, that kind of rage. I felt embarrassed.

"Sorry, Earl."

"It's all right. You're entitled every once in a while. The Good Lord didn't make us perfect."

I smiled. "Especially in my case."

"Now I'm gonna tell Corrina you'll be there."

"I know, I know. Swedish women are real dangerous to disappoint."

He smiled again.

"*Real* dangerous."

I was on the way back to my hotel to clean up when I saw Ham with the buckboard. He was just going around to the back of Zang's Emporium, the biggest general store in town.

I was just naturally curious.

Far as I knew, he didn't *own* a buckboard, number one. And number two, why did he *need* a buckboard.

I went down the alley and parked myself on a nail keg outside a carpentry shop. I stayed under the shade of an overhang so Ham wouldn't see me.

He spent a good half hour in the store.

When he came out, he had a big stogie in his mouth and had nudged his derby back on his head, the smart-boy way Easterners like to wear theirs sometimes. He was giving an old negro orders in his high-pitched voice.

It sure seemed like a lot of stuff.

Now I had to wonder not only about the buckboard but about the merchandise. Where did Ham get the money?

Working out at the Rutledge mansion sure didn't pay him that kind of bounty. The old negro moved with painful arthritic precision.

Ham, playing out his role of importance, chided the old fellow every few minutes to hurry up.

I sort of felt sorry for both of them. The old man was too old to be working and Ham was embarrassing, trying to sound like a general in that squeaky voice of his.

The old man loaded blankets, a lantern, a shotgun, ammunition, field glasses, dry food, canned food and a box of dynamite on the back end of the wagon.

Ham just stood there watching, big thumbs tucked into the pockets of his vest, stogie blazing away in his mouth.

When the old man was done, Ham clapped him on the back and then dismissed him with a wave of his hand.

The old man went back inside.

Ham walked around to the front of the wagon, climbed up and drove away.

I spent the rest of the walk back to the hotel thinking about the dynamite.

At first, it didn't make any sense. Why would you need dynamite to kidnap a young woman? She sure wasn't going to put up *that* much of a fight.

Then I realized what he was doing and it made sense to me. The girl wouldn't put up that much of a fight but the posse would. They'd rush the cabin for sure. And Ham and Callie and Earl were smart enough to get ready for them by arming themselves with sticks of dynamite.

You throw out a stick or two of that, and the posse would forget about rushing the cabin real quick.

I figured she'd be blond, being of Swedish descent and all, but she was dark-haired.

I also figured she'd be dowdy. I'm not sure why. Just something Earl had said during one of our conversations. But she was slender and quietly pretty in her gingham dress.

The two boys, Karl and David, had the blond hair and blue eyes of the Swede. They were stout boys of ten and twelve and they mostly conversed by rolling their eyes at each other every time one of us adults said something stupid—which, apparently, was pretty often.

We said a long and very reverent form of grace. And then dug into the roast beef and potato pudding and fried apples.

The inside of the house was as nice as the outside, which was adobe and sat on a foundation of uncut stone. There were two floors, the bedrooms upstairs, the downstairs two big rooms with a fireplace and hard-packed dirt floors. The lamplight gave everything a glow. I wondered what it would be like to have Nora beside me at a mealtime like this.

"You're sure a good cook, Corrine."

"Why, thank you, Sam."

"She's good at everything," Earl said. "You couldn't ask for a better woman." He was drunk. I'd known it the minute I came through the door. I remembered him talkin' about havin' a beer earlier today. He was giving warning, I guess. To the world and to himself. He was going to go off on a tear. Earl always had an edge when he drank. He managed to look friendly as hell but he could go off at any time. I'd seen him beat several men half to death in prison on the nights when somebody snuck in whiskey. I wasn't sure Corrine knew he was drunk. That might be one of the reasons the boys were rolling their eyes, the fact that their stepfather had tied one on.

She laughed. "Earl does go on."

"You know I mean that, sweetheart."

She reached over and touched his hand. "I know you do, Earl. And I appreciate it."

I felt envious, even knowing that Earl was a hypocrite. He had a good life here. A good woman. I felt lonely.

"So do you like our little town, Sam?" she asked.

"Very much."

"I just wish he'd find himself a decent woman and settle down."

"Maybe God hasn't whispered in his ear yet, Earl."

"That's so."

"Earl always likes to say that people only change their lives when God whispers in their ears."

"Well, I'm ready," I said.

"Really?" she said.

"Really. Earl and me—well, we had some rough times in the past, as you know. Now that I see what Earl has done with his life—that's what I want to do, too."

He hit Karl so hard backhanded that the boy went spilling over backwards, his knees coming up and raising the whole table an inch or two off the floor. The gravy boat spilled.

Earl was up and dragging Karl to his feet before the table had quite settled to earth again.

He threw him against the wall and started shaking him so hard the pictures on the wall began dancing.

The back of Karl's head kept slamming against the wall.

"Earl!" Corrina cried.

"You stay out of this, woman!" Earl said.

Karl's eyes rolled back white. Corrina had started to get up from her chair but then sank back down.

"You're right, Earl. He shouldn't have been acting up that way!"

Then the youngest son was around the table and jumping on Earl's back, trying to stop him from hurting his brother.

It was scary, the way sudden violence always is. I saw the old Earl here—the uncontrollable temper, the animal rage. Sometimes in Yuma he'd get so mad he wouldn't be able to remember it later, like he'd been drunk, even if there'd been no drinking.

"Leave him alone, Earl!" David kept screaming.

In having to throw David off his back, Earl had to stop slamming Karl against the wall.

Karl slipped to the floor.

I got in it, then.

"God dammit, Earl," I said.

I grabbed David's shoulder and pulled him off Earl's back.

Earl turned around, faced me and swung at me. I ducked and he missed.

I backed up toward the table and he flung himself at me.

I fell into the table. I could hear dishes smashing against the earthen floor. And Corrina screaming. And David sobbing that he couldn't wake Karl up.

If there's a hell, it's going to be like that, a vulnerable woman crying and scared for her two young children while her husband tries to destroy everything in sight, out of his mind, beyond any sort of reason or compassion. Dishes breaking. Furniture being knocked over. Sobs. And the unending curses of the madman.

Earl swung at me again.

This time, he caught me on the side of the jaw. It wasn't a clean punch but it did a pretty good job of stunning me.

His second punch caught full on in the stomach.

I didn't have any illusions about holding my own against Earl. Few men could.

That's why I had no qualms about what I did next, which was to grab the milk pitcher, a heavy quart container made even heavier with milk. And when I got my chance, I angled it right at the side of his head, right at his temple.

I broke the pitcher in two when I hit him. Milk sprayed everywhere.

He cursed and charged at me, his head soaked with milk, but he was going on pure instinct, because just before he reached me, he dropped straight down in front of me, unconscious.

"He goes off sometimes," Corrina said quietly.

"The bottle?"

"Yes."

"I thought I smelled it on him."

"Something's eating on him lately."

"He hasn't said what?"

"No," Corrina said. "At least not to me."

"Your boys hate him?"

"Only when he's drinking. Otherwise, he's been a good father to them." Then, "He say anything to you?"

"No."

"It's not a good job for him."

"The law?"

"He tries to save souls."

I almost smiled. He'd convinced her, too.

"That's what he says."

"He goes back there with them prisoners, sometimes three, four extra hours a night, and reads them the Bible."

After Corrina had tucked in the boys, we'd carried him to bed. Between his whiskey and the milk pitcher, he'd be sleeping for a long time.

We sat in rocking chairs in front of the dead fire.

"He always have trouble with the bottle?"

"Pretty much," I said.

"I've seen him on his knees weeping, he was so remorseful the next day. He's a through and through Christian and I know the Good Lord will forgive him."

"We all need a little forgiveness, I guess."

"Are you a religious man, Sam?"

"Not so's you'd notice."

"That's a shame."

"Yes, sometimes I think it is."

From upstairs, I could hear a sudden shout.

"That's Karl. He always has nightmares after Earl beats him. I'd better go look at him."

I nodded.

When she came back and sat down, she said, "Would you tell me if you knew?"

"Knew?"

"About what's botherin' him so much."

"If I knew. Yes, I think I would."

She started crying. Put her face in her hands and started crying.

I went over and stood next to the rocker. I stroked her head and said, "It's all right, Corrina."

"I'm sorry."

"Nothing to be sorry about."

She put her head against the back of the rocker. "He's such a good Christian man otherwise."

"Maybe the Lord will help him."

"I ask every day for that help, Sam."

"I'm sure you do."

"I've even told the Lord to take ten years off my life if He needs to. Take ten years off to trade for Earl being sober."

I'd never heard anybody say anything like that and I wanted to hold her, just hold her for saying it because I'd never known you could love anybody that way.

"You're sure a fine woman."

She smiled up at me and patted the hand I'd put on her shoulder. "Oh, I've got plenty of failings, believe me."

This time, the cry from upstairs was even louder.

"I need to check on him, Sam."

"I know. I need to go, anyway."

She stood up.

I couldn't help myself. I put my arms around her and held her. I felt as if I were holding an angel. I'd never thought of a woman like that before. Her whole sweet prairie soul transfixed me there, it was so pure, almost holy, somehow.

And then I went and spoiled it with a hard-on.

She must have felt it because she gently pushed away from me.

"I really need to go check on Karl, Sam. You're sure a good man. Thanks for being such a good friend to Earl."

And then she was rushing upstairs, and I was letting myself out the front door.

Chapter 12

There were no eyes in the sockets and the nose had been cut away to just a bloody hole now . . .

Her mouth was open wide in a scream that would remain silent for all eternity.

There was blood all over her chest. But I didn't look there very closely. I didn't want to see what they'd done to her there.

Her face was bad enough . . .

Then I woke up.

I half-jumped out of bed and walked over to the hotel window and rolled myself a smoke.

Dawn was still a whispered promise of light behind the mountains . . .

Who had cut her up that way didn't matter.

What mattered was that she had not only been murdered, she'd been mutilated . . .

In prison there was this old guy everybody laughed at. For a nickel, he'd tell you about your dreams, what they meant and what you should do about them. Nick, his name was. Most of the cons thought he was crazy. But I'd listened to Nick carefully. He wasn't crazy and he wasn't a faker. And he wasn't hard to understand, either. A lot of what he said made good common sense.

You start having dreams, say, about your wife back home. And in the dreams she's always in bed with some other guy. Now, that isn't any kind of proof that there's anything going on. But then you watch for other signs, too, Nick would always say. The letters that seem a little distant; not talking about her daily life much anymore, hiding something.

Sure, a guy could just imagine things like that, and a lot of guys do. It's natural when you're behind bars that way. But between Nick interpreting your dream and the letters you get, you got a true reading of the situation.

So what did my nightmare mean?

To me, it was pretty obvious. Something was going to go wrong with the kidnapping, and Nora was going to get killed in the process.

I needed to talk to Callie. Tell her what I'd learned. Just lay it out for her. Tell her not to go through with it.

I finished my cigarette and went back to bed.

I got up at eight o'clock.

There was an old fart using the tin tub. I had to wait till nearly nine to get my bath. A colored kid lugged the hot water up from downstairs.

In the meantime, I went over what I was going to say to Callie.

Mostly, that she was going to die, too.

I'd tell her about the nightmare. And make up a part about them being killed, her and Ham, while they were trying to escape with the money.

Callie would listen to reason. She had to.

I wanted to stay a long time in the tub. If this was nighttime, I'd have brought along a copy of *The Police Gazette* and a stogie.

Parking your ass in a tub of steaming hot water is the best way I know to relax.

The wagon didn't leave for the mansion until about nine-thirty every morning.

The first place I checked was Callie's hotel room.

I felt as if I was a messenger of God. Maybe I couldn't save her soul—only she and God could do that—but I could save her body.

The second place I checked was Ham's hotel room. He wasn't around either.

The next places I looked were the cafés. I hadn't realized before how many there were. They weren't in any of them and nobody had seen them this morning.

I went back to Callie's hotel.

"You see her when she came in last night?"

"I come on at five, sir," the heavyset bald man told me. "Five A.M."

"Was she in her room?"

"I would assume so sir." He was getting irritated.

"That's where you'll find most people that time of day. In their rooms."

"But you don't know that for a fact?"

"I don't tuck them in at night, sir."

"You let me have the key?"

"And what key would that be, sir?"

"To her room."

"I couldn't do that. No, sir. No way. The manager would kick my ass around an entire city block I did anything like that."

I shoved my hand in my pocket and came up with a nice round shiny dollar. "You could buy yourself a nice drunk with this."

"Yessir, I sure could. But I could buy myself an even *nicer* drunk with *two* of 'em."

I dug in and got out a second one. "Her key?"

"Yessir."

He went to a long green metal filing box and began flipping through cards marked with room numbers.

When he came to the one he wanted, he jerked the card out. The extra key was taped to the card.

"We have to be very careful with these."

"I imagine."

"They lose theirs and we lose ours, we're shit out of luck."

"I'd say so."

"We had that happen a couple of times." He made a face. "Had to buy all new locks. The manager wasn't happy."

I loved our early-morning chat—maybe a maid

would appear with tea and crumpets—but right now all I could think about was the key. I put my hand out, palm up.

"You'll be careful with this?"

"Yes."

"*Very* careful?"

It was like taking the Scout pledge or something.

"Very careful."

"And bring it right back?"

"And bring it right back."

"All I can give you is ten minutes."

"That's all I'll need."

I was halfway up the stairs when he shouted at me, "You remember your promise. People give their word around here, we take it very, very seriously."

"How nice for you."

The hall smelled of tobacco smoke, tobacco spit, piss, come, sleep and rain that had soaked into the boards.

Most of the residents were out for the day. They were drummers, most likely.

The closer I got to her room, the clearer the scent of her perfume became. It made me kind of sentimental. She'd been wearing this fragrance the first time I'd ever seen her.

All I'd ever wanted was for her to be the good Callie instead of the bad Callie. But somehow it'd never worked out that way.

Now we were enemies and I didn't like that at all.

I knocked with a knuckle.

Silence.

I knocked again, and again silence.

If she was sleeping in, then she was probably hung-over and wouldn't hear me no matter how loud I knocked.

I used the key.

Just then a man came down the hall.

I felt like a robber, hunched over her door with a key I shouldn't have had.

He gave me a little salute as he passed by. I smiled and let myself in.

The room was a tiny box. There wasn't even a closet. Just a metal pipe to hang her clothes on. The window overlooked a dusty sunshine-blanched alley where two calico cats stood washing each other with quick pink tongues, indifferent to the entire cosmos.

She was on the bed in the clothes she'd probably worn last night. Whoever had hit her had caught her just above the left temple. You could see the blood and the scabbing in the hair.

Her hands were little fists. Her eyes frogged out from their sockets. Her mouth was twisted in pain. Her bowels had gone, the way bowels do when somebody is killed suddenly. I remember seeing a man get hit by a train in Omaha once. His bowels went even before he was quite dead. He looked embarrassed there in the last few seconds of his life. Right up to the very end, I guess, we're social creatures.

There wasn't anything I could do for her.

I spent the next twenty minutes going over the room.

I didn't find anything that looked suspicious.

I pulled up a chair and sat down and just stared at her.

I wished I'd been nicer to her the last time we'd been together.

I didn't even care about her being unfaithful anymore. I don't suppose she ever really loved me, though she said she had. But I think she cared about me. Maybe even cared about me a lot. Cared about my opinion, I guess, more than anything—my approval of her, since she got approval from so few people.

It's funny that she'd die on May 7, 1893.

It sounded wrong.

I don't know what date would've sounded *right*. But this one just sounded *wrong*.

You never know the time or place or circumstance.

They put you in a hospital and you've got influenza or pneumonia or something like that, then it sounds *right* when you die. You're in the proximity of death when you're sick like that, and especially when you're in the hospital.

But when you're just sitting in your hotel room and minding your own business and somebody you trust comes in—you could see that nobody had had to jimmy the door—that's when it gets scary.

Because it means that just about anytime, anywhere, under any circumstances, whenever death wants to swoop down on you—

You can die May 7 or June 23, August 17 or December 25, or any other time death wants to drop in.

I wondered where Ham was.

Probably on a train bound west.

Probably feeling like shit.

Guilty and scared.

Passengers smirking at him because of that high-pitched voice of his.

I felt sorry for her and sorry for him. And then sorry for myself.

Because I wouldn't get my chance to play hero.

I'd come up here to talk her out of it. To tell her that things could go wrong. To tell her that this could be the one thing she wouldn't be able to wriggle out of.

Ham had talked her out of it for me.

"Earl here?"

"He's talking to a prisoner, Sam."

"Mind if I wait?"

"Be my guest. I'm just doing some paperwork."

The sheriff's office was sleepy this time of day. Just the one deputy in the office. Just the wall clock tocking. Just a frantic fly looking for someplace interesting to land, just like the rest of us.

I wondered if Earl knew already. Maybe Ham had told him what happened before he'd abruptly left town.

But, no, unlikely. Earl might not have let him go. Ham wouldn't have wanted to take that chance.

"Hey," Earl said when he came through the door. "How are you, Sam?"

"Fine. Wondered if we could go for a walk."

Earl winked at his deputy. "If I didn't know better, I'd say ole Sam here has come courtin' me."

"Sure sounds that way to me, Sheriff."

"You bring me any flowers?"

Then he looked at my face and gave up his jokes. "You just let me talk to Mike here a little bit and I'll be right with you."

"Guess I'll wait outside and roll myself one."

"Roll one for me while you're at it."

I nodded good-bye and went outside.

I rolled a couple, leaning against the front door. Not even the pretty girls could hold my attention for long.

Earl came out and I handed him his cigarette.

"Thanks."

We walked. We both lit up. We didn't say anything.

"I'm a little embarrassed about my scene at the house the other night."

"That doesn't matter anymore, Earl."

"I've asked God for forgiveness and my wife and sons for forgiveness and now I'm asking you."

"I forgive you."

"I appreciate that, my friend."

He looked humbled. He really did. I wasn't sure he could put on that good a show. Humility was a subtle and very special emotion. I think he was really feeling it. That and the drunkard's worst enemy, remorse.

"I look into Corrina's eyes and see the disappointment there and I—"

But this wasn't the time for his sorrow. "Callie's dead."

He stopped walking. Looked at me. "What the hell're you talking about?"

"Just what I said. She's dead."

"How?"

"Somebody hit her over the head with something heavy."

"My Lord."

"Let's go sit in the park."

We found a bench on the far side of the bandstand. In the shade. The butterflies, the same blue as the cloudless sky, dipped and soared and showed off for us.

"Does anybody else know?"

"Just the killer. I left her up in her room."

"Anybody see you go in there?"

"Some drummer."

"Maybe he'll think *you* did it."

"She's been dead for a while. You'll be able to tell that by looking at how the blood's dried."

He stared out at a dog rolling in the grass, trying to roll the fleas off him. "I wonder if she ever loved me," he said.

"She didn't love either of us. But she liked us."

"I'm glad I met Corrina."

"And I'm glad I met Nora."

He shook his head. He wasn't listening to me. "Callie. Dead. I just never thought of her bein' *able* to die."

"Yeah. I know. She was like a force of nature."

"I wonder if she would've ever settled down."

"I doubt it."

"She wasn't a bad woman."

"In some ways she was."

"Callie," he said. "What a shame." He shook his head again.

"I guess that's the end of your plan, huh?"

He didn't answer at first. Still lost in his thoughts. Then he looked up at me and said, "What plan?"

"Kidnapping Nora."

"You still pushin' that piece of bull roar, Sam?"

"C'mon, Earl, won't hurt to admit it now. You were in on it with them."

The punch came up from somewhere down in the Louisiana bayou and came all the way across to catch me hard and clean on the side of the face.

It had such force that it blinded me for almost a full minute.

Not that I had time to count off the seconds. Because another punch, this one all the way up from the Gulf of Mexico, caught me square on in the mouth and knocked me off the park bench.

All I could do was crawl blindly around in the grass and hope to escape another punch.

Earl decided to surprise me. He didn't punch me any more.

He switched to kicking.

He got me once, twice, maybe three times—to tell you the truth I'm not sure—high up in the ribs.

I pitched forward, pain shooting up in my chest. I started rolling back and forth in the grass, pretty much like the flea-infested dog had.

"You ever say that again, Sam, I'll put you in the hospital."

"You may've done that now."

"Oh, hell, I went easy on you and you know it."

Then he reached down and helped me, none too gently, to my feet.

"I didn't know a darn thing about the kidnapping except what you told me, Sam. It's important that you believe that. And it's important that you believe I've given myself to the Lord. I want you to believe those things so maybe you'll change, too, someday. The way I have."

And I believed him.

On both matters. The kidnapping. And the Lord.

"Get me down to the river, Earl. I don't feel so good."

The water helped. So did the puking.

I lay on my back on the grass, my hat shading my face, enjoying a cigarette that tasted good if I didn't move my arm too fast. Those rib kicks still smarted and would for some time.

"So who you reckon killed her, Sam?"

"Ham."

"I knew you was gonna say that."

"Who else woulda killed her?"

"How about that friend she met in the city barn you told me about?"

"It was Ham."

"Why Ham?"

"'Cause he loved her?"

"Sure. 'Cause of the way he loved her and the way she didn't love him."

"Oh."

"She could be pretty mean to him. About his voice especially."

"That voice. I'll never understand why the Man Upstairs give him a voice like that. People laughin' at him all the time behind his back. You ever watch his eyes when he figures out that somebody's makin' fun of him?"

"Yeah."

"Never seen eyes that sad," Earl said.

"Me either."

"He was like that when we were kids. Those sad eyes."

"So he killed her."

"He's my stepbrother."

"I know."

"And I feel responsible for him." He dragged on his cigarette, exhaled. "Where you reckon he went?"

"Hopped a train."

"Hope he had a little money."

We sat there for a little while, then I said, "I had it all figured out."

"Had all *what* figured out?"

So I told him my stupid dream. About rescuing Nora and being the big hero. About how old man Rutledge would invite me into the family and then make me a land baron or a railroad tycoon or a silver scion. Or something.

He laughed.

"You been readin' too many of them books of yours."

"Yeah, I suppose."

"Anyways, kidnapping like that, just about anything can go wrong."

"Yeah."

"Half the time, the person what gets kidnapped gets killed without the kidnappers even intendin' it. It just seems to happen."

"Yeah."

"So maybe Ham did you a favor," he said.

"Yeah, maybe he did."

"Life is sure a strange business."

"It sure is."

"It don't last that long and not a minute of it makes sense."

"It sure don't."

"Not unless you've got God to talk to."

"I couldn't handle a sermon right now, Earl. I'm sorry."

"Aw, that's OK, son. I'm all sermoned out anyway. I just want to sit here and watch the river and think of Callie. She was quite a gal."

"Yeah."

"I was sneakin' up to her room sometimes."

"I know."

"You saw me the other night, didn't you?"

"Yeah."

"You wouldn't tell Corrina, would you?"

"Nope."

"The sins of flesh. Sometimes they're mighty hard to resist. I only done it four times. Now I'll have it on my soul for all eternity. It'd just break Corrina's heart."

"I reckon it would."

"Poor Callie."

"Yeah," I said, "poor Callie."

So that's what we did till you could see the mid-afternoon shadows start from the banks and spread across the face of the muddy river.

Sat there and thought about Callie.

And then he said, "Better go get her before the flies do."

"I'll pay for a decent funeral."

"That'd be nice of you."

"She just got too smart for her britches, pushing Ham around that way."

"Sure looks like it."

Nothing had changed.

The room was exactly as I remembered it, and so was Callie. Being a lawman, Earl spotted the jewelry box right away. "Ham take anything?" he asked.

"Don't know. Didn't seem to."

"Maybe I can keep him from hangin'."

"How?"

"I know a few judges."

"Oh."

He wrote some things on a note and then took it downstairs to the front desk.

I sat on the chair next to the bed.

A couple of times, I reached out to touch Callie. And then stopped myself. I didn't want to remember her flesh this way.

I killed a couple of flies and then I opened the window higher and sat down again, for some reason staring at the cheap little jewelry box.

And then I remembered the false bottom.

I heard somebody working himself up the stairs. I figured it was Earl. I hurried to the box.

Damned thing broke off my thumbnail getting it open. But it slid back. The false bottom wasn't big. There was an indentation you could hide one item in. The item in there now was a plump emerald ring surrounded with what appeared to be diamonds. It belonged on the equally plump finger of a duchess or dowager. Unless it was paste—and I was no judge of jewelry so it very well could have been—it would be worth a lot of money. A whole lot.

Where would Callie have gotten a ring like this?

All I could think of was her mysterious friend at the barn. I'd never known who he was. Earl swore it wasn't him.

This ring was likely worth more than Callie would ever get for the kidnapping. According to *The Police Gazette*—and I know a lot of people laugh about that particular magazine but it has a lot of interesting information in it—most kidnappers get an average of $40,000. If this ring was real, it had to be worth at least half that much.

Earl was coming through the door. I dropped the ring into my pocket.

He looked at the open false bottom on the box.

"What's that?"

"Her special hiding place."

"Find anything?"

I showed him the empty indentation. "Nope."

He looked back down at her. "I really loved her at one time. Maybe as much as I love Corrina. But in a different way."

"Yeah, me, too."

"I always figured she'd give it up someday, that life of hers I mean. And settle down and raise her some kids."

"She would've had beautiful kids."

"Lord Almighty, can you imagine what those kids woulda looked like?"

"Especially the girls."

"They woulda broken your heart."

There was a huge black fly on her white Irish forehead. He went over and slapped it violently. Then flicked its dead weight away with his finger.

"I sent the clerk to my office. They'll get the undertaker over here and everything."

"What about Ham?"

"I'll check the railroad and the stage. But you're probably right, Sam. He's probably long gone."

"I wonder what broke him." I stared down at Callie as I spoke.

"He loved her too much. It probably just dawned on him in that second that he could never have her. No matter how much money he could offer her, no matter what kind of security, no matter how good a husband he was—he couldn't ever have her. At least not the way he wanted her. So he just went crazy and killed her."

"I guess that can happen."

"It sure can. Especially over a woman."

The undertaker came. I didn't want to watch him work.

I stood in a saloon for half an hour.

I didn't talk. Just sipped beer. I didn't even listen in on the conversations around me.

I kept thinking about Callie and it was kind of confusing. Nora was the woman I'd waited my whole life to have.

Yet Callie kept tugging back at me. She was a whore but there was a sweetness and a playfulness and a decency about her sometimes that almost made up for all the bad things she did to a fella.

I went over to the church and sat in a back pew. I didn't pray or anything. I just sat there. I liked the smells. The incense, mostly, but the votive candles smelled good, too. And the way the sunlight dappled the stained glass and the bare altar.

Callie used to go to mass a lot and I always wondered why, a whore like her.

An old priest walked arthritically down the center aisle to the back of the church. He waved to me and I waved back.

He stopped and said, "You look troubled, son."

"You think a whore can get into heaven, Padre?"

He smiled. "A lot worse people than whores have gotten into heaven, son. They just have to spend a longer time in purgatory than most of us."

I didn't believe any of the religious stuff but still his words made me feel better for Callie's sake.

I lay on my bed the rest of the day, rolling cigarettes, and rolling Callie's ring over and over in my fingers.

I wondered where she'd gotten it.

At dusk, I went to the café and ate. I was just finishing up when Earl came in looking tired and old. Even my baby face was starting to look old these days.

"Is Corrina going to be mad, you eating in a café like this?"

He shook his head. "No, she's not. She was the one who told me to come down here."

"What happened?"

"The other night. When you were there."

"Still mad, huh?"

"More disappointed than mad. Mad I can handle. Disappointed, I don't have a chance."

He had the special, the steak and potatoes, same as I'd had.

While he waited for it, he drank the scalding coffee and said, "I asked around about Ham and Callie."

"Oh?"

"Every night, people in the hotel said. Every night they got into it. Several people said they weren't surprised at all that he killed her, the way the two of them went at it. Couple of them said that it was kinda funny in a cruel way. The madder he'd get, the higher his voice'd go and they didn't know whether to laugh or cry."

"Poor Ham. And poor Callie."

"Nobody seemed to catch what the arguments were about, though. They said they always started late at night and went for a couple hours at a time. Neighbors'd stomp on the floor and yell things out the window to get 'em to shut up but nothin' worked. The clerk, he told me he went up there with a sawed-off a couple of times. He said they'd calm down but go right back at it after a while. So when he *did* kill her, they didn't think it wasn't nothin' special. Just figured it was another night of arguin' and they'd pick it up again the next night."

I wanted to show him the ring. I don't know why I didn't. I'd told him everything else.

Was I thinking of stealing it for myself?

Big town like Denver, if it was the real thing, I could get a lot of money for a ring like that. I surely could.

The ring seemed to throb in my pocket. There were

a lot of tales of magic rings. This wasn't magic. But it sure did seem to have some kind of hold on me.

"I'm also still tryin' to figure out who she met in the barn that night you followed her."

"Why?"

"Maybe he can shed light on why Ham killed her."

"Oh."

"And I'm just plain curious. Aren't you?"

"Yeah; yeah, I am."

"I'll find him. You can bet on that."

"But you still think Ham's the killer?"

"Sure. Don't you, Sam?"

"Yeah."

The woman brought his dinner. Manners weren't his strong suit. In Yuma he was legendary for the noise he made while cleaning his plate. He could teach hogs a thing or two. The thing was, I never got used to it. You figure, a couple of years with a mate who slurps and smacks his lips and snorts and grunts, you'd get used to it. But you never do. I never did, anyway. Every single night, I wanted to take a shotgun and fill him with lead just because he made all those aggravating noises.

He made all those same aggravating noises tonight.

"It's funny, though."

"What is?"

"That jewelry box."

I gulped.

"What about it?"

"The false bottom being open."

"*I* opened it."

"You did?"

"Yeah. I told you that."

"You did?"

He was sheriff now. Not Earl anymore. Sheriff Earl. I could see the skepticism in his eyes.

"You think I took something from that box, Earl?"

He looked at me so hard it went clear through the back of my head. "You're the only one who knows that, Sam."

"I didn't."

"Well, if you say you didn't, then you didn't."

He didn't believe me.

"She showed me once. How the false bottom worked."

"I see, son."

"And so while you went downstairs, I got bored and decided to open it up."

"I see."

"And it was empty."

"I see."

"And it just so happened when you walked back into her room, I was fiddling with it."

"I see."

"Will you quit saying 'I see'? That drives me nuts just the way your eating does."

He smiled. "I still make a lot of noise, huh?"

"Noise? Didn't you see those people plugging their ears?"

He smiled. But not much.

"God, Earl, I didn't take anything."

"Then the matter's closed."

"But you still don't believe me."

"It's your soul, son. How you conduct your life is up to you. Not me."

He finished up his coffee and then picked up his hat. "Got some more rounds to make before I head back home for the night."

"She going to let you back in tonight?"

He cinched his hat good and tight on his head. "She told me I could sleep anywhere I wanted—in the barn."

I don't think he was fooling.

Chapter 13

It was next morning just before noon when I saw John Rutledge and three of the men who worked for him ride into town.

They all wore suits and Stetsons and carried rifle scabbards. All but Rutledge wore mustaches.

They hitched their horses in front of the sheriff's office and went inside. I noticed that they didn't look around, the way men do when they come to town, or say a word. They went straight inside.

They were just coming out the sheriff's front door when I saw them again. This time Earl was with them. He didn't look happy. If he saw me, he didn't let on. He carried a sawed-off.

They mounted up and rode out. No fuss, no hurry. Just serious and important men doing serious and important business.

I wasn't the only one who noticed them.

Man standing next to me said, "Somethin's sure up."

"Wonder what?"

"Maybe at the mines. Heard there was some of them union bastards out there again. You know how John is about them union people."

"What can he do about 'em?"

"Word I got is he hired some man from Kansas City to kill the last two that started talkin' to the miners."

"How he'd get away with it?"

The man snorted. "How you *think* he got away with it? He jes' said he wanted it done and it was done."

All up and down the street you could find little groups of people watching them and speculating on what they might be up to.

Later that afternoon, when I was playing pinochle in one of the saloons, somebody came in and said the deputies wouldn't say anything at all under strict orders from Earl.

After a time, I got a chilling feeling about Nora.

What if Ham decided to kidnap her anyway? He'd need money if he meant to escape, and he obviously had everything planned out.

I got out of the card game and went to the bar and drank myself three beers in a row, all the time daydreaming.

Maybe there was still an opportunity to save her.

I'd rubbed them smooth, those daydreams—rubbed them smooth and dreamed so devoutly.

What I hadn't counted on was thinking of Callie every once in a while.

It was funny, all the times I hated her and wanted to kill her, now all I could summon up was the good Callie, not the bad one.

I was heading back to my room when I saw her there in the twilight. She had on a simple riding outfit and a flat-brimmed hat.

She ground-tied her horse and went directly inside the sheriff's office.

Not long after, she came out and started to mount up.

I was there next to her horse in moments.

"Nora. Nora, it's me, Sam."

Her hat was pushed back on her head. Even in the half-light, you could see how hard she'd been crying, her eyes puffy and her nose red.

"Hello, Sam."

"Nora, what's wrong?"

"I can't talk about it, Sam. I'm sorry."

"But you look so upset."

"Just say a prayer, Sam. That's all I've been doing all day. Saying prayers."

The deputies came around the side of the sheriff's office, leading two saddled mounts. They recognized me and nodded.

"No time for talk now, Sam. Sorry," one of them said. He rode lead, turning his horse so that it pointed west.

She surprised me by reaching down, holding out her

hand. I took it, held it for a moment. "Just say a prayer, Sam."

"I will, Nora. I will."

Then she was gone, silhouetted against the purple-salmon, pink-and-gold sky. The snow on the mountains was pink. A sentry owl announced the falling night as the air filled with the scent of the foothill pines.

I didn't sleep well that night. Kept waking up. Thinking of how Nora had taken my hand.

I could actually *feel* her hand there in the darkness. The dancing gal noise would fade and the casino noise would fade and the player-piano noise would fade and I'd be left there in darkness and silence with just her tender hand to hold.

The next day was rainy and damp and cold. I went to the café for breakfast, then picked up a couple of magazines and some tobacco and headed back to my room.

About all I had to do was plan where I would be headed next. This place had the feeling of the jinx on it now, Callie dead and all, and I wanted to get out of here as soon as I could.

In the afternoon, I went to the church again. I sat in the last pew and listened to the rain pattering on the roof. The smells were good and clean again, the incense and the votive candles.

The old priest didn't come. I sort of missed him. There was something regal in his presence. His cassock and the way he carried himself said that there was order and justice in the world after all.

I went and had a few beers late in the afternoon and then went back to my room and lay down and slept through till the following morning. Gunshots woke me.

I ran to the window and looked down.

Earl was way down in front of the sheriff's office. In the middle of a circle of men. They looked agitated, eager.

I jerked my clothes and gun on and took the stairs two at a time.

The wagon traffic was just now starting for the day. Yesterday's rain had left the streets muddy. Some of the horses had mud all the way up on their faces.

I saw a couple of men hurrying away from the crowd. One of them said, "I'm gettin' my rifle and I'll meet you back here."

I grabbed his arm. "What happened?"

"What happened? You been asleep or somethin'?"

"Yeah, as a matter of fact I have."

I was ready to hit him. He saw it and backed off.

"The Rutledge kid got kidnapped."

"Oh, shit," I said.

So Ham had taken her after all. Too much money to resist.

The man tugged his arm away and took off with his friend.

I walked over to the group encircling Earl. There were farmers, merchants, drifters, the undertaker, two parsons, a few cowboys and one or two men who looked like hobos.

"We'll meet back here in twenty minutes," Earl was saying. "We'll divide up into four groups. Remember to bring water and dry food for a long day. And no alcohol."

Somebody laughed.

Earl looked aggrieved. "I know it sounds hypocritical, me sayin' no alcohol when I've got a problem with old John Barleycorn myself. But this here's got to be a serious posse. We owe that to Mr. Rutledge. His kid's life may be at stake here."

A couple of men still smirked but their friends nudged them with their elbows. How could you make fun of a man who was so honest about his drinking problem?

"So remember. Back here in twenty minutes. Then we divide up."

The men, at least those who were planning to go, hurried away. In addition to weapons, they'd probably bring bedrolls, just in case. That was a lot of stuff to organize in twenty minutes.

I went up to Earl.

"He did it, huh?"

"Oh, he did it all right," Earl said. "May God be with him."

"I suppose he thinks he needs the money."

Earl looked at me, sad and disgusted. "He don't seem to understand about kidnapping, does he? They hang you for it. Robbin' banks, robbin' trains, even some kinds of murder—you can sweet-talk your way past a jury if you've got the right kind of attorney. But not kidnappin'. Because everybody thinks how it'd feel to have your *own* kid snatched like that."

"Especially one as nice and sweet as Nora."

His head jerked back. "Nora? What the hell you talking about?"

"Ham kidnapping Nora."

"Ham didn't kidnap Nora."

"He didn't?"

"No. He kidnapped Cal."

"What?"

"Yeah. Cal rode home from town here pretty drunk as usual and that's when Ham nabbed him. Left the ransom note on the front steps of the mansion."

"Cal? Why would he take Cal?"

"Probably 'cause he couldn't figure out any way to get Nora. He probably had that all worked out with Callie, but with her dead, he had to do the best he could. So he took Cal." He smiled coldly. "Cal's a bad kid, no doubt about that, a drunkard and a bully and a big-mouth. But Rutledge still loves him. He's his own flesh and blood. He'll pay whatever Ham asks him to."

"How much did he ask for?"

"Thirty-five thousand dollars."

"How's Ham going to get it?"

"Right below Lightning Cliff. Rutledge or his appointed man's supposed to drop it off the cliff. Ham'll be waiting below. With Cal. Everything works all right, Ham'll give the kid back."

"When's all this supposed to happen?"

"Nine tomorrow morning."

I calculated the distance from the kidnap cabin to Lightning Cliff. It wouldn't take Ham more than forty-five minutes to ride there. Meaning he'd spend the night in the cabin with Cal.

There was still a chance for me. All my little-boy dreams of someday being a hero were going to come true. Long about dusk, I'd be paying Ham a visit.

"I'm going to kill him and just get it over with."

"Ham?"

"Yeah."

"I owe it to our mother."

"Oh?"

"She'll want to come up for the trial. It'll be too much on her. She's sickly and old as it is. I think she always loved Ham a little better than she loved me. Not that I minded. He was the squeaky wheel with that voice and all and how the other kids picked on him."

"Maybe you won't get the chance to kill him."

Earl shook his head. "One thing Ham's not taking into account. There's only one trail down to the rocks below the cliff, so nobody can get down there after him. But somebody can come across on the water."

"A canoe?"

"Yup. Or just swimming. The water isn't that rough upstream there. Downstream is where it's bad."

"And that's going to be you?"

"It should be me. By rights. I want to make sure he's dead for our ma's sake." Then, "You going along?"

"Just want to pull some things together."

"You still thinking about Callie?"

"Yeah," I said. "Yeah, I am."

"So'm I." He frowned. "Poor kid. Had a couple of dreams—sad dreams—about her when I was sleepin' in the barn last night."

"Corrina ain't let up yet, huh?"

"Usually takes her three or four nights. Swedes got a mean streak. Don't let them mild blue eyes fool you."

He looked over at his office. "I better get my own gear together."

He put out a hand. We shook. He walked over to the sheriff's office and went inside.

The rain-sloppy trail would slow me down some but I figured I could get to the cabin by dusk.

I was just walking my horse out of the livery when I saw, down the street, the unmistakably graceful figure of Nora hurrying up the broad steps of her church. She quickly slipped inside.

I walked my horse back into the livery and told the man I'd be back in a while, had just remembered something I needed to do.

I went into the church after her. I felt like a criminal. I didn't belong here. It was three times as big and fancy as the Catholic church. And cold. Without the sweet scent of incense.

There was a tall pulpit and a beautifully carved wooden altar with a huge cross set against the back wall. The choir loft was also outsized. A vast organ sat on the north side of it.

She knelt in the front pew, her head bowed.

I was suddenly nervous, wondering if I should even be here. Despite the romance in my head, I barely knew her. Maybe she'd resent me being here. She'd know I'd followed her.

I worked my way slowly up the long center aisle. It seemed to take forever. You could hear my spurs. The shabbiness of my clothes, my dusty boots, my Colt . . . emblems of my not belonging.

I knelt in the pew behind her.

She didn't look back at me.

I bowed my head. I even said a prayer. For Cal. And then for myself. That I could pull this off. So much could still go so wrong.

I said, "Nora."

Her head came around quickly. And then her hands. She sat in the pew and took both of my hands in hers. She'd been crying pretty hard. I thought of Corrina the other night. Her pale face so red from tears.

"They took Cal."

"Yes, I heard."

"What if they kill him?"

Her tears came in small gasps.

"They won't."

"But a lot of times—a lot of times they kill the person even if they don't need to."

I wondered about Ham. I didn't know him well.

He'd killed Callie. He might have killed other people before her, too.

"They just want money, Nora. That's all. Then they'll leave."

"I'm just glad my mother isn't here to see this. She always worried about kidnappers when we were very young. And my dad—at his age this could kill him. If we get Cal back all right, then Dad should be fine. But if we don't—"

Sad child. That's what she looked like. Those huge brown eyes of hers. That sweet mouth. A sad child.

"I had better pray, Sam."

"I just wanted you to know that I'm thinking about you."

"Just say prayers, Sam."

"That's what I've been doing."

"Cal wasn't very nice to you. But he's really a decent boy. He really is. He just thinks he's important sometimes and it goes to his head."

"If we both pray, he'll be fine, Nora. I'm sure of it."

She leaned forward and kissed me on the mouth. Not a deep kiss but a real one. I could taste her warm tears. I got a hard-on right there in church. I was glad we had a pew between us.

"I really like you, Sam. But I guess you could kind've tell that."

"Then you sure must be able to tell how much I like *you,* Nora."

"Just pray for him, Sam. Pray very hard."

She turned around facing the altar again and then bowed her head.

I got up quiet as I could. I walked on tiptoes to the back of the church. My shabby clothes were bad enough. I didn't need to make noise, too.

The livery man said, "There ain't gonna be any saddles left in town, the way things're goin'."

"Posse?"

"Yup. They catch those sons of bitches, they'll hang 'em right on the spot."

I didn't have any doubt about that.

"He ain't a real nice kid, I'll grant you that. But he's one of our own. And you can bet there ain't a man in that posse don't want to kill them kidnappers."

I swung up in the saddle and rode out of town.

The trails were muddier than I'd expected. The horse lost his footing a few times, slipping. Once, rounding a curve with a deep gully below, he scared the hell out of me. I could see me and my plan tumbling down that gully. But maybe I wouldn't care by then. Maybe I'd be dead by then. And so would the horse . . .

If nothing else, the rains had made everything shine. The mountains and the land looked store-bought new. Even the birds seemed to sing a little louder and truer.

I had a real sense of ascending. The air thinned out. The temperature dropped some, despite the sunshine. And I could see how thick the clouds were covering the peaks of the mountains. I was still in the foothills.

Reaching the tops of the mountains would take a lot longer than I had.

There was always the chance that somebody was going to beat me, to the cabin and to Ham and Cal.

The cabin wasn't all that difficult to find, especially to somebody who knew this area of the mountains. Fact is, they might think of it right off. But there was a lot of land to cover so they might still overlook it, think that maybe Ham took Cal to a place farther away.

The scent of her tears stayed in my nostrils. I wasn't thinking about Callie anymore. Now there was only Nora.

She liked me. She said that to me. She liked me. No coyness, either. I've never been a fan of coyness. Women should speak bluntly, just like men. She liked me. Bluntly. No cuteness, no games.

By the time I got him back home, even Cal would be a fan of mine. He'd have to be, me rescuing him and all.

I kept on climbing.

The first bullet came close enough to me to smell. Stench of discharged metal; stink of gunpowder.

I threw myself to the ground, rolled over behind a boulder. I'd plucked my Winchester from its scabbard and was in good shape as far as firepower went.

The shooter was up behind a cluster of small boulders. He was sweating me out a little. He hadn't fired for three, four minutes. Trying to make me nervous.

I saw the very tip of his black hat move along the top edge of a boulder. The way his hat bobbed, I could tell he was walking on his haunches. He might well be as scared of me as I was of him, though I didn't know why, because he had all the advantages.

Another few minutes went by.

And then I saw him.

A little more of the black flat-crowned hat bobbing up and down. Only this time it was bobbing behind a stretch of boulders that were laid out vertically. He was sneaking down the mountain toward me.

He wasn't very good at it. In fact, he stumbled once and it made me smile. His hat went ass-over-appetite behind a boulder and then bobbed into sight a few minutes later. He'd probably had to chase it downhill and dust it off before putting it back on his head. A vaudeville routine out here in the middle of nowhere. I was a most appreciative audience.

He had one big problem.

He was about to come to the trail.

There was a gully behind me and no place for him to hide once he crossed the trail, except behind a scrawny, hairy jack pine. His idea was good in theory. Sneak up beside me. But he hadn't thought it through.

I got ready for him by angling myself on the far side of the boulder so that when he got near the trail I'd be waiting for him. There was a huge, jagged spire of rock near him. It stood right next to the trail. This was the only possible place he could shoot from. By now, even a dummy would know that there was no way to come up beside or behind me.

All I had to do was wait.

He gave me enough time to play out a hand of solitaire.

I wondered what the hell he was up to.

And then I found out.

My friend had another friend. And the other friend had, cleverly enough, come up behind me. I had no idea he was there until it was too late.

"I could put a hole the size of a silver dollar in your forehead," he said. "So I'd put the gun down and stand up real nice and easy." He was short, dumpy, dressed in a ragged and faded flannel shirt, a pair of baggy work pants held up by a pair of sorry red suspenders. He was twenty at most.

"Who the hell are you?" I said.

"Who I am ain't important. It's who *you* are that matters. And you're one of them."

"Them? Who's them?"

"The kidnappers."

"What the hell you talking about? I'm out here *looking* for the kidnappers."

"Yeah? Then why aren't you with the posse?"

"Why aren't *you*?"

He looked uncomfortable. I'd asked him a question he didn't want to answer.

His friend came then. I didn't know his name but I recognized his face. He'd spent some time idling in the sheriff's office. He seemed to know Earl pretty well.

"Aw, shit, Tim," he said. This one was tall, gaunt, with a three-day growth and a slow left blue eye. I was never quite sure what he was looking at.

"What? What's wrong, Mike?" Tim said.

"This here's Earl's friend."

"The sheriff's?"

"Yeah."

"Aw, shit. You sure?"

"Sure I'm sure. Shit." Shook his head. "Give him his gun back."

"What if he shoots us?"

"We got guns, ain't we?"

"Yeah."

"And there's two of us against one of him?"

"Yeah."

"So he ain't gonna shoot us. And we ain't gonna shoot him. Sorry, Mr. Conagher."

I shrugged. "Nobody got hurt. That's all that matters."

"I should've recognized you."

"You should have field glasses is what you should have."

"Can't afford 'em, and the old lady'd kick my ass if I brought a pair home. We ain't hardly got no furniture. And the youngest kid's always sick. She'd kick my ass for sure."

"Right up to his neck. You should hear her. She's about the crabbiest lady in the whole Territory."

"Well, at least I'm married, Mike. More'n you can say for yerself."

"I'll be gettin' married one of these days, Tim. Don't you worry 'bout me."

Tim laughed and winked at me. "He'll be gettin' married soon as that whore he sees gets rid of her disease."

Mike said, "Maybe Sam here'll want to ride with us."

Nice little box canyon they took me in. No way I was going to lead them to the hideout. But maybe I'd look suspicious if I outright turned them down.

"Which direction you headed?"

"West," Tim said. "Over near the Indian land."

"Old Tim says we got nothin' to worry about. Course he ain't never seen nobody scalped like I have."

Tim shook his head. "He claims that this here fella he knew got scalped and lived through it. Now, how big a crock is that?"

"Actually," I said, "I've read that that's happened."

"Fella lived through a scalpin'?"

"Yep."

"Aw, bullshit. Where'd you read it?"

"*Police Gazette.*"

"*Police Gazette.* Who believes any of the bullshit they print in there?"

"Well, a lot of people sure seem to," I said, "the way they sell copies and all."

"Aw, hell, they just sit back there in New York and make that shit up."

"See what it's like bein' around him?" Mike said.

"Even when you present him with the evidence like you just done—with *The Police Gazette* and all—he'll still swear you're full of beans."

"OK, I'll go collect me a Commanche and we'll let him scalp you and see if you're alive and kickin' afterward."

"You see what I got to put up with?" Mike said earnestly.

I was sure looking forward to spending an afternoon's ride with them. I sure was.

You could sense the Commanches but not see them.

They were in the pines and hiding up on the ridges and skulking along riverbeds. This was their land and they weren't happy about us being here.

Why these two bright boys had figured that the kidnappers would take Cal here I couldn't understand.

Taking Cal here would double their difficulty. They'd not only have to watch out for the posse, they'd have to watch out for the Commanches. It was hard to tell which presented a worse fate—a blood-raged posse or a blood-raged pack of warriors.

Also, these boys never quit arguing.

The longest debate concerned a hermaphrodite horse they'd seen at a circus in Denver.

"Had a pussy and a cock both," Mike said.

"A pussy and a cock," Tim said. "That cock was no more a cock than the man in the moon."

"Now yer sayin' the man in the moon's got a cock?" Mike continued the sophisticated repartee.

"This dumb bastard'll believe anything," Tim said as we rode toward a mesa. "You shoulda seen that pathetic thing. The cock was a fake."

"If anything was a fake," Mike said, "it was the pussy."

"See what I mean?" Tim said. "He thought the pussy was a fake."

Such delightful traveling companions.

I had a couple of ideas but decided against them.

My horse could go lame, but that wasn't easy to fake.

Or I could come down with a sudden attack of stomach flu. *You boys go on ahead of me. I'll catch up after I'm feelin' a little better.*

But dumb as these boys were, they'd be just smart enough to figure out what I was doing. And they'd get all suspicious. And wonder why I was dropping back all of a sudden.

So when the shadows grew long, and the air began to cool, I said, "Guess here's where we say good-bye."

They'd been arguing about which one of them had eaten the most flapjacks at the last county fair. Mike claimed to have et thirty-six; Tim claimed to have et forty.

"Aw, bullshit," Mike said.

"Bullshit yerself, and you never et no thirty-six neither."

"Fuck if I didn't."

"Fuck if you did."

"Bullshit."

"Bullshit yerself."

"Well, fuck you."

"Well, fuck yerself."

It wasn't going to be easy to tear myself away from these boys, they being so charming and all, but somehow I'd manage.

I said, again, "Guess here's where we say goodbye."

From our particular perch along the trail in the foothills, we could see a dusty, winding stage road below. A creek ran to the right of it, the sky painting it blue. A pretty picture.

"How come yer leavin' fer?" Tim said.

"Need to get back to Texas."

"Texas ain't in that direction. Utah is."

And he was right. I'd never been real strong at math or directions.

"You didn't let me finish, Tim. I've got to see somebody in Utah first, *then* go to Texas."

"Oh."

"That's a sure long trip," Mike said.

"Ain't *that* long a trip," Tim said. "Good weather'n all."

Fortunately, they didn't argue about how long my imaginary trip was going to be.

"You don't want none of that re-ward, huh?" Tim said.

I shrugged. "I had myself one day to look for the

kidnappers. And that's just what I spent. One full day. Now I have to ride on."

"Gal waitin' for ya, is she?" Mike said.

"I wish. Nope. My uncle died and I've got to take a look at the old farmhouse so the banker can try to sell it."

It was a pretty good story for spur-of-the-moment.

"What'd he die of?" Mike said.

"Old war wound."

"Oh yeah, which side was he on?"

"Union."

Tim said, "Well, I guess I don't give a shit if you ride with us no more. Fact is, if I'd have known you had Yankee kin, I wouldn't've let you ride with us in the first place."

"Never mind him," Mike said. "My pappy wore the blue, too, mister."

"We woulda won if the North didn't have all them slaves fightin' for 'em."

"Slaves? Shit, the Yanks was just better fighters was all."

And so I left Indian country and my friends with their jovial, relaxing disagreements. I couldn't afford to be around them any longer. I just might be tempted to shoot them in their sleep.

It took me till dawn to find the cabin. Tim and Mike had led me a long, long ways from my real destination. I hadn't slept. There wasn't time.

There was an unnatural quiet around the cabin.

There wasn't even any birdsong. It was as if something terrible had happened here, something so terrible it had silenced even the birds.

I took my field glasses out and looked the place over carefully. My main concern was riding into a trap.

You might have posse members hiding in the trees behind the cabin, just waiting for somebody to ride up. There could be an exchange of gunfire between Ham and the posse and I'd be right in the middle of it.

Or, no posse, a nervous Ham might pick me off with his Winchester.

The sun rose quickly. The day birds began singing. That made me feel better. Night fled. The pine trees changed from silhouette black to green, and the mountains took on their own gritty immortal colors.

I tried to see into the cabin through the only window but Ham had a piece of burlap nailed over it.

There was only one way I was going to get down there and that was to sneak down.

I got back on my horse and rode higher up in the foothills so that I could scrabble down the shale hills behind the cabin.

I kept expecting to see some of the posse hiding out in the pines or behind a sizable boulder. Eighteen hours had elapsed between the kidnapping and now. Somebody was bound to think of this cabin.

Twice I thought I saw the glint of a rifle barrel in the sunlight. But both moments of panic proved to be nothing.

I ground-tied my horse in the pines and started my way down the hills. I had my Winchester and my Colt. I wasn't going to take any of Ham's bullshit. I understood that he wanted money to escape with and I didn't blame him.

But this was my only chance to ever win Nora. To make something out of a life that had been nothing but daydreams and failures.

I was going to take Cal back home.

I reached the cabin. Put my ear to the back wall. The wood was so weathered, I could hear right through it.

If anybody had been saying anything.

Silence from inside.

The earth smelled good as I crouched there. Rich black soil. The aroma made me close my eyes, just enjoy it for a moment. My nerves were bad. A sleepless night always makes me jumpy. Like too much coffee.

Silence still.

Maybe they were asleep.

If Cal was tied up and gagged, Ham could get at least a few hours of shut-eye.

I haunch-walked around to the front of the cabin. Ham'd dug a small latrine and they'd given it good use. Flies had declared a national holiday.

I looked around the hills and the pines. I had the sense again of somebody watching me. Posse members, most likely.

I stood up. Knee bones cracking in the stillness.

My Winchester might be too awkward bursting through the door the way I planned.

I set it quietly down on the ground.

Took out my Colt.

I'd go in shooting, smashing the door in with my shoulder. The pine door didn't fit inside the frame right anyway. It had shrunk some and the hinges were rusted. Breaking through it wouldn't be any trouble.

Between the gunfire and the door flying open, Ham'd be too confused for the moment to fight back much.

I walked back several feet. I needed a good run at the door to make sure it would bust open when I needed it to.

It came open a lot easier than I thought it would. The pine was in bad shape but not nearly as bad as the hinges.

The door flew inwards and I followed it.

I put a shot straight ahead, a shot to the left, a shot to the right. I was an easy target, hunched there in the doorway. But there was no alternative. I went in or I didn't.

Nobody returned fire.

The cabin was a one-room thing with a potbelly stove, a counter for cans and dry goods, a paint-scabbed rocking chair, a dusty yellow pile of news-papers and enough rodent shit to feed the fire for years to come.

Everything was dusty, dirty. I sneezed.

All this I got at a glance.

What I didn't get without some serious study was Cal. He was sprawled on his back across the lone bed, which was really more of a cot than anything.

It was the way he was sprawled, I guess, as if a giant hand had flung him across the bed. His arms were out at a scarecrow angle and his right leg was bent so oddly it looked to be broken.

His eyes were open and he looked pretty sad. He had the brown eyes common to the Rutledge clan. But these had assumed a look of very un-Rutledge-like beseechment. They seemed to be begging, in fact. Begging the gods, perhaps.

Or, more likely, begging the man who had done this.

Please don't do this. I have money. Don't you know who my father is?

All the arrogance would have been gone from his voice there at the last. I probably would've even felt sorry for him.

Maybe Ham just went crazy. Just put the two bullets in Cal's forehead because he couldn't stand the punk anymore.

Then he'd put a couple of bullets in Cal's chest, too. The blood had pooled and was now in the process of drying. The stink was coppery, harsh.

"Sam."

The voice spooked me. I spun around, went into a gunny's crouch, fired twice.

At nothing.

When it had spoken my name, the voice seemed to

be directly behind me. Just where I'd pumped the two slugs.

But actually the voice had come from behind where the door still hung on one hinge. The door kept him hidden from sight.

I didn't have to wonder who the voice belonged to.

He was propped up against the wall. The shooter had done a good job with him, too. From my count, he'd taken three shots in the chest. There might be more. His eyes had that repellent gleam you see in some slow-dying farm animals. Repellent, I suppose, because you can imagine that same gleam in your own eyes someday.

His derby was still on. All the blood, all the mess in this cabin, and his damned derby was still on. And jauntily, too.

He tried to speak, couldn't.

I ran out to my horse and got my canteen.

I forced Ham to drink it slow. He kept grabbing at it with those outsized, powerful hands of his, nearly swiping it from me, even in his condition.

"You crazy bastard, why'd you kill him?" I asked when he handed the canteen back.

His jowly cheeks were dirty. You could see where his tears and his sweat had streaked them. He shook his massive head.

"I don't know what you mean, Ham."

There was a strange, terrible sound trapped in his throat. I guess it's what some people call the death rattle. But it didn't sound like a rattle. More like a fatal wheeze.

Maybe sitting him up straight would help.

Moving him wasn't easy. I got my arms under his and tugged with everything I had. I could feel my balls being sucked up into me. Ham was the kind of guy who could give you a hernia.

It took me several tries, him not helping at all, before he was sitting upright.

And it was just then that my horse neighed.

That was all I needed. Cal was dead and somebody had followed me.

"I'll be right back," I said.

The first thing I did was yank my Winchester from its scabbard. Then I grabbed the field glasses.

I went around back. That was the most likely place visitors would come.

They'd sneak down the shale hill just as I had.

Except there was nobody there. Nobody I could see anyway.

I went back to the front of the cabin. Spent five minutes checking out the down slope in front of the thin lines of pines in front.

Nobody there, either. And they'd be a lot easier to see in front than back.

Sweat covered me like glue. My clothes stuck to me and I felt filthy. I hadn't been in town long, but a man can get used to bathing and changing into clean clothes. I listened to the birds and the other forest animals. No sounds of urgency. No sounds of sudden intrusion.

Horses get spooked a lot and there's rarely an explanation. I climbed the shale hill to my animal, stroked him a few times and went back to the cabin. Not his fault that I'd taken his noise as a warning.

This time, I thought Ham was dead for sure. He was still sitting upright but his head was at an angle and his features were tight and closed. Even his derby was off now, the brim of it sitting in a small puddle of blood. I looked at his bloody chest for any sign of rise and fall. None.

I knelt next to him. Took off my kerchief and soaked it in canteen water.

Washed his face. It took a while but he finally responded. His eyes flew open. I could tell he didn't know where he was. Or who I was. Maybe he didn't even remember who *he* was.

"Ham."

"Huh?"

"Listen to me."

"Who is it?"

"Don't you recognize me?"

"I can't see."

"Oh, shit. It's me. Sam."

"Sam. She shot me in the head."

He'd given me two puzzles at once. Who "she" was and a reference to a head wound I hadn't seen.

"Where's the head wound?"

"Behind my left ear."

It was there all right. It didn't look that bad—more superficial than anything—but then I wasn't exactly a medical expert.

And then he said, "It's getting a little better. I can see a little bit."

He was a strong bastard, especially when you considered that he was dying. No way I could get him to a doctor to take care of the wounds and the blood loss.

"Who shot you?"

"*She* did. I told you."

I couldn't help but sound irritated. "Who is 'she,' Ham?"

"Cal's sister."

"*Nora* shot you?"

"Yeah. Fuck, I'm really gettin' weak here, Sam. I gotta get to a doc."

"But why would *she* shoot you?"

His breath was coming in gasps now.

"Cover everything up. She paid me and Callie to kidnap her brother. She said she just wanted to scare him into growin' up a little."

"How much she pay you?"

"She paid down with this ring she gave Callie. She said it was worth ten thousand dollars."

I dug in my pocket. Brought it out. "This ring?"

He squinted. "Yeah. That's the one. Then she said we got to keep all the kidnap money. She said she would even help us escape in a railroad car."

The blood started from his mouth and nose then.

It was easy to imagine a black cowled figure sitting

quietly in a chair across the cabin floor. Just waiting for his moment. He wouldn't have long to wait now.

"So that's who Callie was seeing all those nights when everybody thought she had a beau?"

"Yeah. Nora Rutledge. They was plannin' all this out."

The cough came. And the blood got worse. "Took me till just a while ago to figure it out, Sam."

"Yeah?"

He nodded. "Nora kills me'n Callie so we can't ever talk and then she kills her brother and gets his half of the estate, too."

I kept thinking it was impossible. I kept thinking of pure, sweet Nora. I kept thinking of the soft way she spoke to me; of the shock and pleasure I'd felt when she'd taken my hand.

"She didn't like you no more, Sam. Callie didn't."

"Yeah, I know."

"She wasn't as bad as you thought, Sam. I'll bet God lets her into heaven."

I smiled. "She'll sweet-talk him."

"I love her so much, Sam."

He started crying and I felt like shit for him. I felt like shit for everybody, in fact. Everybody but Nora Rutledge.

Callie had done many dirty things in her life, but she'd never killed her brother for money.

"I think she woulda married me someday, Sam. I really do." The funny thing was, his voice was much deeper now, almost like a regular man's. Here at the very last, his voice finally changes. Life is just so strange sometimes.

And then he was crying again.

And I could feel his body turning.

Maybe his soul was leaving. I'm not sure what it was. But his skin felt different and the hands were no longer strong.

"Would ya do me a favor?"

"Sure, Ham."

"Put my hat on me."

"Sure."

"I wanna look good in case Callie's looking down."

So I put his hat on him and damned if he didn't look jaunty again.

"So long."

"So long, Ham."

"I'll say hello if I see Callie."

"You do that."

And about two seconds after Ham's head lolled to the right and he died, they came tramping through the open door, their guns drawn and Tim saying, "You stay right where you are, Sam. If that's what your name really is."

"We figured right away you was one of the kidnappers," Mike said.

"I figured right away," Tim said. "You didn't figure out shit."

"Well, I figured it out right *after* you did then," Mike said.

Tim lowered his repeating rifle at me and said, "As

an official deputy, I now arrest you for the kidnapping and murder of Cal Rutledge and claim the re-ward for me and my partner here."

"Fifty-fifty, remember," Mike said.

"Yeah, but I was the one who figured it out first, so I'm entitled to more."

"You sumbitch. You dirty sumbitch. I knew you was gonna pull somethin' like that."

But Tim was more interested in me than Mike at the moment.

I was still haunched down next to Ham.

Tim gave me a good and bloody kick in the mouth. Then he got the cuffs on me.

Chapter 14

I've read a lot of good articles in *The Police Gazette*. In one, the posse lynched five men off the same tree all at the same time.

The articles do a good job of describing the anger of the mob and the fear of the men who are about to die. A few of them are still cocky right up to the end but most of them just get real quiet. You can see in their eyes how terrified they are. A couple of them cried, I guess. Just bawled like little kids, bawled and pleaded and begged. But it did no good. They got killed anyway.

The one thing that articles never mentioned was the embarrassment.

A couple miles outside of town, Mike rode on ahead to tell Earl that they'd found me with the dead bodies of Cal and Ham, their surmise being that I'd killed Cal just because I hated him so much and that I'd killed Ham so I wouldn't have to split the ransom.

There were at least two things wrong with their case. The first being that I certainly didn't hate Cal bad enough to kill him. I'd never killed anybody in my life and wasn't sure I could unless my life literally depended on it.

The second thing was, if I was the wily criminal they claimed I was, why would I have killed Ham now, before I had the ransom money?

Wouldn't it have been much smarter to send Ham after the money, let him risk getting caught by men hiding somewhere nearby. And then—if he got safely back—take the money for myself and kill him?

But the $15,000 reward had taken away their good judgment, assuming they'd ever had any . . .

Anyway, I was going to tell you about the embarrassment.

So there I was, my horse being led into town by Tim, my wrists handcuffed to my saddle horn, and my face pretty badly beaten up from Tim's kick job.

At least two hundred people were in the street waiting for me. It was like a real mean-spirited carnival was in town. There was hooch being drunk openly, and men were firing shots into the air, a little Mex band was playing something festive on the porch of the Dirty Flirty casino, and a lot of drunken men were openly groping a lot of drunken women.

And in every eye was malice and hatred and violence.

I kept looking for a kind face as I passed through the crowd on horseback. But I saw not a one.

I felt embarrassed, humiliated, more so than I ever had before in my entire life.

All my life I'd felt outside the normal stream of humanity. Something kept me separate, different.

But now I wasn't just strange. I was bad. And that was what I saw in their faces, even in the faces of the children.

I was an outcast and deserved their wrath.

The community was only doing its sacred duty, putting to death a person whose very existence was a humiliation, a joke, to the men and women of the town.

Somebody hit me with a piece of rotten fruit.

Then somebody hit me with a piece of rotten vegetable.

Then a man hawked up a good one and goobered me on the side of my face.

A little boy gave me the finger until his ma saw him and slapped his hand down. Then she took up the cause in a more civil way, screaming "Killer! Killer! I can't wait till they hang you!"

And all this time the Mex band was playing some really catchy tunes.

Up near the porch where they played, there were six or seven couples dancing.

A pair of cowboys, so drunk they had to wobble forward to do it, grabbed at me and tried to pull me off my saddle. Their drunkenness had blinded them to the handcuffs.

Tim just kept guiding me steadily toward the sheriff's office. From what I could see of his face in occasional profile, he wasn't playing to the crowd. He just wanted to deliver me and collect the ransom from old man Rutledge.

Mike was enjoying his new celebrity. He kept doffing his hat and grinning at the ladies.

He even tried twirling his six-shooter, the way they do in those Wild West shows that come to town every once in a while, but he dropped it on the ground and a genteel older lady had to return it to him.

The jail was starting to sound good to me.

I might have to listen to all these people drunkenly taunting me from the street, but at least I wouldn't have to see them. And eventually they'd have to go home and sleep it off. Wouldn't they?

A nice sweet jail cell.

That showed how bad my senses had been scrambled.

There was no such thing as a nice sweet jail cell.

Earl stood on the boardwalk in front of his office. He had his sawed-off dangling from his right hand.

He just watched it all.

He was a commonsense man and common sense had to tell him that trying to disperse this mob was not a good idea at the moment. Too much hooch, too much rage. He'd go from lawman to enemy instantly.

When I got a good look at his face, I could see he was avoiding my eyes.

Everybody knew we were old friends. He couldn't afford to show any sign of favoritism.

"Get him inside," Earl said.

Tim and Mike obliged.

As they uncuffed me and then dragged me down from the saddle, Earl went out on the edge of the boardwalk and looked over the crowd, making sure that nobody tried to rush me.

"It's all pretty much over now, folks."

"He killed Cal," somebody shouted.

That's another thing about mobs. They'll stand up for anybody if they're drunk enough. Cal had probably treated nearly everybody in this mob like hell at one time or another.

But in the liquor and frenzy of the past twenty-four hours, all was forgotten and forgiven.

By the end of the day, Cal would be portrayed as a man who'd spent most of his time tending to the needs of the deprived children and communicating directly with God. Yes, the same Cal Rutledge who had cheated at cards, bullied lesser men into fights and arrogantly intimidated people by virtue of his father's name . . . now we'd be talking Saint Cal Rutledge.

More fruit, more vegetables, more slurs came raining down upon me.

Earl stayed real easygoing.

"This is a nice town, and you're all nice folks. Let's not go and ruin that now, all right? We're taking him inside and we're going to question him and we're going to find out everything we can about the kidnapping. And as soon as we learn anything definite, we're going to let you know everything we do. And that's a promise."

The six khaki'd deputies, heavily armed but wearing patient smiles, had apparently come out the back door and fanned out.

They came at the crowd from all sides, gently breaking them up, pointing them in various directions. A few complained, of course, but the deputies were able to handle even the real troublemakers.

Then I was inside and Earl was grabbing his large, jangling ring of keys and leading the way through the door to the cells in back.

The nice sweet cell didn't look nice or sweet. It looked cold and shadowy and narrow, a forerunner of the grave itself.

I wanted to talk to somebody and fast. Give my side of things.

Earl opened up the cell door and pushed me inside.

"Earl," I said. But he wasn't listening.

He just slammed the door, locked it and walked back up to the front of his office.

They gave up around suppertime.

I guess even name-calling and threatening folks can get tiresome, even behind ungodly amounts of beer and rotgut liquor.

A couple of the epithets I'd never even heard before. At least my incarceration was educational.

I just kept thinking of how stupid I was, and how ashamed I felt for calling Callie a whore.

She hadn't been lying. She hadn't been a whore in her heart. Maybe she laid down too easy sometimes but she'd never have killed her own brother.

That's the part that made me feel so stupid. How I could have been taken in by Nora and called Callie a whore.

I saw Nora in her church clothes. I saw Nora at the picnic table that day slicing cake for all of us workers. I saw Nora holding my hands so tenderly in hers.

And that was when I realized the trouble I was in.

All the way back into town I was just thinking I'd get Earl alone and we'd talk and I'd explain what had happened, what Ham had said and all, and Earl would go to Mr. Rutledge and tell him.

But nobody would believe him.

Beautiful, gentle Nora.

Certainly not Mr. Rutledge.

He'd just say, *Have a look at that angelic face of hers, Sheriff. You telling me that a girl like that could be mixed up in something like this?*

It was like somebody telling you that the nun who'd just walked by spent her nights dealing crooked poker and putting out for twenty-cents a flop.

Nobody was going to believe me.

They'd already convinced themselves I was guilty.

And they were going to hang me.

.

And they weren't necessarily going to wait for the circuit judge to make it nice and neat and legal either.

I finally drifted into a light sleep around suppertime, seeing the first of the evening's stars between the bars of my cell's high small window.

"And you were going to be the hero?"

"Yeah. That was my plan anyway, Earl."

"That's why you didn't tell me about this?"

"Yes."

"So you set her free and then turn Callie and Ham in?"

"I guess."

"What's that supposed to mean, you guess?"

"I guess it means I hadn't thought that part through, I guess."

"Well, you would've either turned them in or let them ride free."

"I guess I would've let them ride free."

"And then you'd be the big man?"

"Yes."

"And old man Rutledge would've showered you with money and his daughter?"

"Yes."

"That's about the dumbest thing I ever heard of."

"It sure sounds like it now."

"The first thing I would've thought of—you being friends with Callie and Ham—was that you were a part of it."

"I can see that now, Earl."

"And didn't you figure out that things usually go wrong in kidnappings?"

"I just figured I could control everything, I guess."

"You guess."

"And now you're accusing his own daughter of being behind all this?"

"Ham wouldn't lie to me."

"He wouldn't?"

"No."

"Sure he would. He'd lie to anybody he needed to."

"But what would be the point? He was dying."

"Maybe he was just up to mischief."

"Not Ham, Earl. He wasn't like that."

"This here ring, you even sure it's hers?"

"The way Ham described it, it's hers all right."

"And she gave it to Callie?"

"That's what Ham said," I told him.

"Ham said, Ham said. Who gives a damn what Ham said? That's what Rutledge is gonna say, and that's what people in this town are gonna say. Who was Ham? Some squeaky-voiced outsider who kidnapped a rich boy. Ham said. It don't matter what Ham said, Sam, and you better understand that darned quick."

"You sound like you believe me."

"What I believe don't matter. It's what I can prove."

"You believe me, then?"

"Quit askin' me that."

"But how else would Callie have gotten the ring if Nora hadn't given it to her?"

"She stole it, that's how. She and Ham working out

at the mansion like that. They could've snuck in easy and taken a whole lot of things."

"You don't walk right into that mansion. There's too many people around, coming and going and stopping and talking. They'd see you."

"Well, that's what Rutledge'll say. That they stole it, people comin' and goin' or not."

"Well, what if it's true that Nora gave it to Callie?"

"How many times I got to say it, Sam? It don't matter if it's true. You always have this little boy sense of things. Probably twenty percent of the men we was in prison with shouldn't've been there. They were innocent just like they said. But they couldn't prove they were innocent and that's all that mattered."

"I don't know why I was so stupid to get involved in this thing."

"I don't know either, Sam. You shoulda come to me."

"That mob this afternoon really got on my nerves."

"They got on my nerves, too. And they're gonna get on my nerves even worse tonight."

"You think they'll be back then?"

"Don't you?"

"Yeah, I guess."

"I expect Rutledge anytime, Sam. He's gonna be hurt and he's gonna be pissed and he's gonna want to kill you hisself."

"I guess I'd be the same way, if it was my son I mean."

"So I'm gonna ask you one more time. Did Ham or

Callie ever mention anybody else in cahoots with them?"

"Not that I can remember."

"Think."

"Nobody else. I'm sure of it."

"I'm not gonna mention Nora to him."

"What? You have to."

"No, I don't. Bad enough his kid is killed. Then tellin' him his daughter was behind it. He couldn't handle it."

"So you're not gonna do anything about it? I can't believe that."

"Just stay calm, Sam. I'm gonna ask around. I'm gonna find out about Nora. But before I go to old man Rutledge, I got to have some hard facts. Ham's word just ain't gonna cut it."

That was when somebody hit the bars of my window with a soft rock that shattered all over my bunk.

He let me clean up and then they brought me food from the café. By this time it was full night and the crowd was full, too.

I lay on the bunk and listened to them outside. I couldn't relax. They scared me. I'd seen what mobs could do.

I thought about Callie and how sorry I was about things. If she just hadn't been so unfaithful all the time, we could've had a good life. Or maybe if I'd learned to just accept the way she was. There was a fella in prison who'd told me that he didn't mind his wife screwing other men the way she did because he knew it didn't mean anything to her. I figured he was lying, but I got to know him over the years and decided he was telling the truth after all. He said the only time it ever bothered him was when she gave him the clap one time and for that he gave her a good stiff beating. But otherwise, he just figured it didn't matter.

I said a prayer for Callie and then I asked her to forgive me and then I thought about Nora some more and I still couldn't figure how anybody could've been that good a liar.

She was part of the dream I'd always had and now the dream looked foolish. After everything that had happened in my life, still dreaming that same stupid storybook dream.

The firecracker woke me up good and fast.

Somebody pitched it between the bars.

I'd been so caught up in my thoughts, facing the wall the way I was, turned on my side comfortable and everything, that I didn't even know it was on the floor next to me till it went off.

I jerked to my feet. A deputy came running back.

"Sons of bitches!" he said.

Laughter. Outside. Kids, it sounded like.

"Little peckers!"

He went straight out the back door.

"You boys git on home! You know I could arrest you for throwin' firecrackers like that! You think it's funny, Billy? Well, you won't be laughin' when that old man of yours beats your ass bloody, lemme tell you that!" He yelled the way riled men always talk to belligerent kids who have the upper hand. "That's right! Run! And you better keep on runnin', too!"

And then he came back inside, feet trompin' and slammin' the door and mutterin' "Little peckers!" again and smellin' of tobacco and sweat in his smart khaki uniform.

"Gonna be a long night," he said, all out of breath.

"Yeah," I said.

"The heat ain't helpin' any either."

I hadn't noticed the heat for a while. But he was right. I naturally expected the temperature to drop with night. But it hadn't dropped much.

My bedclothes were soaked from my sleep and my shirt was stuck to my back and arms. The filthy feeling again. Never again to be cool. Never again to be dry. Never again to feel safe.

"How many you reckon there are?" the deputy said.

I smiled nervously.

"I haven't actually tried to count them."

"I'd say a hundred by now for sure."

"Or better," said a second deputy coming through the door from the office. "There's a whole pile of them down around the casinos. We went down there with sawed-offs and broke 'em up but they're already back again."

"Sure hope Earl can handle 'em," said the first deputy.

The other one nodded.

• • •

Another hour.

It appeared as if the mob from down around the casinos had drifted up to the sheriff's office. The crowd size had at least doubled. Not all of them were ranting at me. Some of it was a social event. People who hadn't seen other people for a time were standing and chatting. The kids ran around, especially the little ones, like it was a church social. You could even see a few teenage romances blooming. So what if a man was in his cell and a few in the crowd wanted to lynch him? Lynch him or not, this moment would pass for these folks, and soon enough it would be forgotten, and they would have long been returned to their ranches and farms and businesses and schoolhouses.

Life goes on.

Every once in a while, I'd stand on my bunk and peer out the window.

This was all right the first couple times. But now they had people watching for me. I was like a carnival act.

I'd peek my head up and they'd throw something at me. A rock. Or rotted vegetable. Or a firecracker that would miss its mark, bounce off the jailhouse wall and then explode on the ground.

The kids loved the firecrackers.

We were having Fourth of July early this year.

I paced. There wasn't much room but I did the best I could. Rolled cigarettes and paced and sweated and every once in a while I'd have one of those nervous spasms, my whole body would jerk, like I was having a seizure or something.

I wanted guns and I wanted dynamite and I wanted nitro.

The kids left around eight-thirty. This was way past their regular bedtime anyway. Of course, a possible lynching was a special occasion.

Easterners despised lynch law. They were always writing books and editorials against it. But it wasn't always bad. Sometimes it was the only way a community could deal with a certain kind of person who was, without doubt, guilty.

The trouble was, sometimes they lynched the wrong person.

I lay on my bunk now, smoking a cigarette.

My impression, from the voices, was that the crowd had thinned some, leaving mostly men, and only those men who were very serious about lynching me.

A couple of times I heard Earl out there.

He always kept his voice reasonable and a few times he even got kind of jokey with them. And they'd kind of back down a little. Not all the way. But a little.

He was good with them.

He reminded them that they had families and responsibilities and hopes for the future. He didn't say it any preachy way either. He just said it kind of slow and natural-like and you could feel his words working.

And then he said, "Somebody always gets hurt when things get out of hand. And it's usually somebody innocent. You remember when ole Curly Evans

got shot in the back by somebody tryin' to shoot the
prisoner? You seen ole Curly lately? Paralyzed from
the waist down. And all just because somebody got all
liquored up and got hisself to feelin' all high and
mighty and went out to do what he thought was a good
turn for his community and left Curly Evans—who
was then, what, twenty-two, -three years old?—crip-
pled for the rest of his life? Now, we sure as heck don't
want anything like that to happen. But I'd sure appreciate it if you'd get on back to your business in the
next half hour or so. Besides, most of us got to get up
early anyway. So stayin' out all night in the middle of
the street's gonna make tomorrow mornin' come awful
early."

The third time he gave this version of the speech, it
actually pushed some on their way.

One of the deputies stood on a milk stool down the
way looking out the bars and said, "Be damned if a
whole bunch of them ain't movin' on down the street."

By the time another half an hour had passed, I couldn't
hear anybody out there.

Earl came back. "Cheated death again."

"I don't know how you do it," I told him.

"I didn't do it."

"No?"

"No. God did."

"Oh."

"I know you don't believe that but it's true."

"I really appreciate it."

He sat on the opposite bunk rolling himself a cigarette.

"Corrina's bakin' you a pie tomorrow."

"That sounds great."

"How you doin'?"

"Scared."

"I think you'll be all right. For tonight anyway. Tomorrow's the weekend. Saturday night's gonna be hellish in town here. It always is. Rutledge's men come in."

"Great."

"I'm gonna ask ole John to rein 'em in. He's the only one what can."

"You gonna tell him my side of things? About Nora?"

"I'm just tryin' to imagine it, is all."

"Imagine what?"

"Sittin' there in his parlor. And me accusin' his daughter of bein' behind this whole thing," Earl said.

"It's true."

"Even if it is."

"Funny thing for a Christian man to say, that the truth doesn't matter."

He took a deep drag on his cigarette, leaned back against the bars, exhaled a long blue stream of smoke.

"Sometimes the truth don't set you free, Sam. Sometimes the truth destroys you. I bet he's seen Nora for what she is all of her life. But he can't afford to admit the truth to himself because it'd destroy him. He has to believe that she's just what she seems to be or the whole world'll seem crazy to him. Here's this sweet innocent girl—only she's not sweet and inno-cent at all. But you lose your belief in her—what you gonna believe in then? Nothin'. There's absolutely nothin' to believe in."

"It's me or her, Earl."

"I know. And that's why I've got to tell him the truth. But I sure am scared. He might just kill me on the spot."

"I'm sorry to ask you, Earl."

He sighed and looked sad as hell there in the jail shadows.

"I know you are, son. I know you are."

Chapter 15

The next day was the hottest yet.

I slept till breakfast then slept after breakfast. The Territorial judge was out of town, so there was nobody to arraign me and nothing for me to do.

Earl brought me some magazines.

"Couldn't find no *Police Gazette*s."

"These'll do just fine."

"I'm ridin' out to see old man Rutledge in a couple of hours."

"You going to tell him about Nora?"

"Corrina says I owe it to you to at least bring it up."

"Bless her."

"It could mean I'm all through in this town. I've got a lot at stake here, Sam. Wife. Kids. House. Friends."

"I know you do, Earl."

He looked at me and shrugged. He looked tired, gray.

"I'll do what I can, son."

"Appreciate it, Earl."

In the afternoon, some of the kids came back.

They stood by the rope corral in the rear and hurled rocks at the back of the jail. Every once in a while they'd call out my name. They didn't bother me much. I mostly read and slept.

Late in the afternoon, one of the deputies said, "The padre would like to talk to you, Conagher."

"The padre?"

"Yeah. The priest."

"What about?"

"You'll have to ask him."

The priest was a beefy, flushed man named Monaghan. He wore a dusty black cassock that must have been like wearing an iron suit in this weather.

The jailer let him in and then locked up the cell.

"You call when you want to leave, Father."

"Thanks, Leo."

The priest sat on the opposite bunk and said, "They'll probably try again tonight."

"Yeah. They probably will." I didn't want to give him the satisfaction of sounding scared.

"They might get lucky, son."

Now I had two people calling me "son."

"They might."

"In which case you want to be prepared."

"You going to give me a gun, Padre?"

"Is that supposed to be a joke?"

"You said I'd want to be prepared."

He waggled a small Bible at me. "I was talking about your soul."

"Oh."

"When's the last time you went to confession, son?

"Never."

"You've never been to confession?"

"Nope. But then that shouldn't be so surprising. I'm not a Catholic."

"With a name like Conagher?"

"I know. Everybody assumes that with my name, I'm a mick. But I was raised Baptist."

"Good Lord."

"So I'm afraid you've wasted a trip."

"I could baptize you."

"It's kind of late, Padre."

"It's never too late, son. Not in God's eyes." He studied me a moment. "Especially not when you're sorry. Are you sorry you killed Cal Rutledge?"

"No."

"You're not sorry?"

"No, I didn't kill him."

"That isn't what everybody says."

"Well, everybody's wrong."

"You could still get into heaven if you'd repent and throw yourself on God's mercy."

"I *am* repenting, Padre. Because there's this woman

and I was wrong about her. She was a lot better woman than I gave her credit for."

"I'm sworn to secrecy. If you want to tell me about Cal, I mean."

"You don't believe me, huh?"

"If you didn't kill him, who did?"

"Nora."

"Nora Rutledge? Are you out of your mind, son?"

"I may be out of my mind, Padre. But I know that for a fact."

"God have mercy on your soul. Telling lies about an upstanding young woman like Nora."

"She wanted Cal's half of the inheritance."

The priest crossed himself. "I am in the presence of satanic forces."

"She's the one you should get to confess, Father."

He went to the cell door and shouted, "Deputy!"

"Though I guess that wouldn't work out, either. Would it, Padre, since the Rutledges aren't Catholics either?"

"Deputy!" the padre shouted again.

He just wanted out of there. Fast as possible. Never to see me again.

Unless it was at the end of a rope.

The deputy came. "You all right, Father?"

The padre glared back at me. "I will be as soon as I get some fresh air."

And with that, the poor bastard went back to his flock.

•   •   •   •

I wasn't so cocky half an hour later when one of the deputies said to the other, "The Rutledge crowd just got in down the street."

"All of 'em?"

"All of 'em plus a few more than usual."

"Great. It's gonna be a long night."

He looked down the row of empty cells to me. "Nothing for you to worry about, Conagher. Earl runs a tight town."

"I know he does. But even Earl can't stand up to forty of Rutledge's men."

"Ain't forty."

"No?"

"Thirty at most."

"Gee, what a relief."

"You'll be fine. Earl would consider it a personal insult to have a lynching in his town."

"Earl back yet?" I said.

"Nope. Still out talking to old man Rutledge, I guess."

"He gets in, ask him to come back and see me."

"Sure thing."

"Leave me a couple rifles while you're at it."

He smiled. "I'll leave you some blasting caps while I'm at it."

There was a gathering up at the end of the day. Not only did the plodding horses sound weary, but so did the wagons themselves. Even the little kids were all yelled out and laughed out and run out and grinned out. They sounded weary, too, and didn't have to be begged to come home, just took a call or two from their moms, all that good food and cool drink waiting for them. And between the bars you could see that the sky was worn out, too. No longer a solid blue but almost a watercolor, too tired for solids now. And the dust motes didn't slide and tumble as they had all day but just froze in the last gleam of the sunlight, just froze and stayed there. It was all like a picture now— a painting—all sound receding and receding and receding and then I wasn't me anymore. I was somebody else or nobody else sitting back in a corner, watching this nobody named Conagher live out his life as time faded and darkened everything in its wake, until Conagher himself and everything he ever saw and heard and felt and knew and aspired to had faded and darkened, too.

And the funny thing was, it wasn't so bad. For just those time-frozen moments there I wasn't scared and Callie had forgiven me and Nora had to face justice and I forgave my folks for running off on me the way they had and everything was right with Earl and Corrina again.

Just the fading day; just the fading day.

He got back just as I was finishing up my supper.

He finished up my chicken for me and then lay down on the bunk opposite and said, "You notice anything different about me?"

"Huh-uh."

"Look closer."

I couldn't see what he was talking about.

"Still can't see it, Earl."

"On my vest."

"Oh."

"Oh? That all you got to say? He tore it right off me."

"I'm sorry, Earl."

"He tore it right off me."

"Because of what you said about Nora?"

"Darned straight because of what I said about Nora. He laughed. He said that was the only thing he could do, the whole story about Nora and all was so crazy. He said he was going to keep me acting sheriff for the next couple of days. But then he was going to get the council to appoint a new one."

"You tell Corrina yet?"

"Yeah. I stopped home on the way back to the office here. Told her everything."

"What'd she say?"

He lifted the hat from his face, looked over at me.

"She said they were going to kill you tonight."

I didn't say anything.

He put his hat back on his head.

"That's why he's got extra men in town tonight. Beef up the lynch mob."

"So he's really going to try it?"

"He's going to do more than try it, son."

I didn't know what to do with my hands or legs. I'd start to stand up then I'd sit back down. I'd start to

scratch my face and then I'd suddenly reach for my tobacco instead. My stomach kept clenching and un-
clenching. My bowels felt cold, sick.

"You sound like there's no way to stop 'em, Earl."

"There ain't."

"You've got some good men."

"Not that good."

"So we just sit here and—"

He sat up, swung his feet around. "You got a
smoke?"

I threw him the makings.

"Must've left mine at home."

He rolled one and got it going and then pitched the
makings back to me. "What size clothes you wear?"

I told him.

"I guess we're generally the same size."

"Why?"

"Because as soon as it's full dark, you're gonna
walk out the back door."

I could hear them out there already. Probably not
more than a couple of dozen. But they were already
pelting the jail with rocks, and occasionally somebody
would call out my name.

"I guess I'm not sure what you're talking about."

"You'll be wearing a khaki uniform same as me and
my guards. You'll keep your hat pulled real low so nobody can see your face much. I'll have a horse all saddled up for you. You'll have a six-shooter and a
repeater in the saddle scabbard. You'll ride out of here
real slow, like you're just going on an errand or some-

thing. Soon as you hit the edge of town, that's when you ride hard. By the time anybody figures out what happened—even my own men—you'll be long gone."

"And you'll be stuck here to face Rutledge."

"Yeah, I guess I will."

"You talk this over with Corrina?"

"Yeah."

"And she said all right?"

"She said it was the only thing we could do and still call ourselves godly people."

"They may think you were a part of it all. Cal getting killed and everything."

"I don't have no choice, son. It's my faith."

I rolled myself another one. Sat back. Watched him.

His hand was trembling as he brought the smoke to his lips.

"You're scared."

"Darned betcha I am."

"You don't have to go through with it."

"Sure I do, Sam."

"I'm not sure I'd do this for you. Ruin my whole life and my family's whole life this way."

"If you believed, you would."

"But I don't believe."

"I know."

"I wish I believed. I *want* to believe."

"Then maybe someday you will."

I felt terrible. You could see that he wasn't convinced he was doing the right thing. Sacrificing so much. He'd worked so hard at building up a good reputation after his prison years. And now it would all be gone.

"They could send you back to prison, Earl."

He smiled bleakly. "They'd have to catch me first."

"It's not a joke."

His eyes burned beneath the wide brim of his hat. He needed a shave and his craggy face was gaunt to the point of looking starved. There was just a hint of the madman about him. He looked as he had in our younger days, when we'd been outlaws and everybody knew enough to walk wide of Earl Cates.

"I know it's not a joke," he said.

"I almost want to talk you out of it."

"I noticed that word 'almost.'"

I took a drag off my cigarette. "Maybe if I could talk to old man Rutledge."

"He'd probably shoot you on sight."

We didn't say anything for a time.

The crowd got bigger. There didn't seem to be any kids tonight. That wasn't a good sign. The carnival air of the previous night was gone. This wasn't as noisy but it seemed a lot more serious.

"Your whole life, Earl. Thrown away."

"It's what the Lord wants me to do."

He stood up.

I started to say something.

"Now shut up, son, before you talk me out of it. I'm gonna get everything ready. You just wait here."

"Earl—I just want you to know how grateful I am."

He smiled bleakly again. "I thought I told you to shut up, son."

There were several night riders in black hoods. A couple of them carried torches. They looked spooky, there at the back of the crowd.

Rutledge's men, cowboys cleaned up for town, filled up the front of the crowd. They fanned out so that they encircled about eighty percent of the sheriff's office and its grounds.

Rocks, bricks, curses.

They started bombarding the jail with all three, almost never letting up.

A few times, one of the deputies would come back to see how things looked from this vantage point. They looked young and scared. To a man, they tried to sound brave. "Not as many of them as I was afraid there'd be," or "Nothing we can't handle with Earl in charge," or "We've dealt with crazier mobs than this one before."

Earl hadn't let them in on the plan. He was sparing them. If it all came apart, they could honestly say that they hadn't known anything about sneaking me out of the jail.

The few times I stood up on the bunk and took a quick look outside, I could see that Rutledge's men had moved to the front of the mob. There were more torches, more shotguns and, in the back, more black-hooded night riders.

They started shouting my name.

It was almost funny. They didn't know how to do it the right way. They were drunk, at least a lot of them were, and so their voices waggled and warbled and didn't sound dramatic at all.

I paced some more.

Every five minutes or so a deputy would come back. "You hear anybody at the back door, you just holler, all right?"

I nodded.

"They'll probably try the front door first. Back door's metal. They'll have a harder time gettin' in."

I wondered how high Earl was going to let everything build.

I wondered if Earl had maybe changed his mind.

I could understand why. Throwing everything away for me. He'd worked hard to change the impression people had of him. And these days he was a decent man. Even if I somehow survived a lynch mob, the jury was likely to find me guilty anyway. There wasn't any place in this part of the Territory where the name Rutledge didn't carry weight.

Maybe he'd just decided I wasn't worth it, and much as I might resent him for it, I couldn't blame him.

There were enough torches now that I could smell their kerosene. And there were enough people so that I could smell the hooch and tobacco and sweat of them.

No Earl.

I was pacing when the bucket of pig shit was thrown at the window of my cell.

It came splashing through the bars, flying and flicking everywhere. I was near the cell door and didn't get much of it.

It was fresh, hot pig shit, too.

The stench on a hot night like this made me clamp my hand over my nose and mouth.

The people in the crowd laughed as one. The carnival was back in town. The midway had just opened for business.

There were a few sentimental, sanctimonious speeches, one good citizen or the other reminding the people of all that Rutledge had done for this community, and what this community owed him, and of what a basically decent boy Cal had been. Sure, nobody would deny that he had a few faults here and there, but overall he was a good Christian boy who meant well. This community, this very group of people gathered here tonight, owed it to Rutledge to avenge the terrible thing that had happened to his son.

"What the hell they throw back here anyway?" Earl said, coming through the door.

"Pig shit."

"Crazy people," Earl said, "why do they think we've got courts?"

"They want to impress Rutledge. Especially his own men."

He sighed. "I suppose." Then, "Here you go, Sam." He stuffed a carpetbag between the bars. "Everything you need is in there. I've got to go back up front. You change clothes real fast and I'll be back."

He started to turn away but I grabbed his sleeve.

"They're gonna find out, Earl."

"I reckon they will."

"Then what?"

He shrugged.

"This is the right thing to do under the circumstances, Sam. That's all I can worry about, just the way Corrina says."

"Well, I really appreciate it."

"I know you do, Sam. I know you do."

I dressed fast. The clothes were just a bit big but looked fine otherwise.

He'd also supplied me with a Colt .45 and a holster rig.

The one thing I didn't have was a hat to go with the uniform. A lot of people had seen my own hat around town. They might recognize it. I needed a different one.

A reverend addressed the crowd then.

You'd expect you could pretty much write a reverend's sermon in these circumstances. How the Lord had given the power of law to elected officials—render unto Caesar and all that—and how we should not therefore take the law into our own hands.

God would not be happy about this.

The reverend said the opposite.

"It's what is in our hearts that matters to the Lord," the reverend said. "If we keep forgiveness in our heart while we are doing our duty here, then there is nothing wrong with hanging this man. If we can honestly look into our souls and see that it is not hatred that drives us, but a simple need for justice, then the Lord will understand and forgive what we're about to do."

In some ways, that was the scariest moment yet. The reverend who claimed that lynching was all right.

The next thing Earl brought me was a hat. Black Stetson with a wide brim flapped low in the front. Perfect for concealing a face.

"You ready?"

"Yeah."

"Don't even look back at me. You understand, son?"

"Yeah."

"There's a mount down by the rope corral. He's all saddled and everything. You march straight to him and get the hell out of here."

I nodded.

"No matter what happens, you don't look back."

"What if they make a play for you?"

"That's my problem. Not yours. You just keep ridin'."

"Earl—you sure all this is all right with Corrina?"

"I'm sure."

"Earl—"

"Don't go gettin' corny again, Sam."

"You're a true friend."

"I'm just doin' the right thing is all. Let's go. I'm gonna walk over to the crowd and start talkin' to them. And meanwhile you scoot away behind my back to the horse corral. You got that?"

I nodded.

"Now remember. Just forget I'm there. Forget the crowd's there. All you worry about is gettin' to your horse and gettin' out of here. Remember?"

I was shaking pretty bad. You get on the edge of a crowd like that, no telling what they'd do. Maybe they'd see the ruse right away and open fire. Or maybe they'd follow me to the rope corral and grab my horse before I could.

Or maybe they'd just grab me and lynch me, the way they wanted to.

He was at the back door. Opening it.

The night air outside wasn't any cooler but it was different in texture and aroma. The pig shit odor was mostly confined to the jail cells. You could also smell perfume and shaving lotion and beer from the saloons. And a round golden Indian moon blazed in the middle of the sky.

I stumbled crossing the threshold and sort of tripped my way out the door, the way they do in those vaudeville shows when the comic makes the funny entrance.

Earl turned a sharp right, toward the crowd.

And I headed toward the rope corral.

I couldn't see the horse. Panic filled me. I looked all over down there. No sign of the horse at all.

And then it strolled calmly from behind a couple stacks of hay bales.

Her essence filled me is the best way I can say it. She was inside me the way I'd been inside her so many times. I could taste her sex and her nipples and her tears and her sweat and the tang of her perfume after she'd just put it on. The good Callie. The Callie I loved. The Callie who used to drag me to early morning mass after she'd cheated on me and say that she wanted to be pure the rest of her life, give herself only to me, and wouldn't I please pray—for both our sakes—that that would come true?

I wasn't even much aware of it really, the horse turning back in the opposite direction and finding its footing and heading in a direction that might very well take me to my death. I guess I didn't think of it that way. I just wanted to tie up loose ends, was the way it came to me. There were things left undone, and how could a fella ride out of the Territory when there were things undone? Neat and clean was the only way I could start my life over; neat and clean, nothing left undone.

A sudden rain stopped after a while, and the foothill trail beneath the pines grew dry. I was able to ride faster.

Not that I had any idea of what I was going to do.

Only of where I was going: the Rutledge estate.

Nora'd be there somewhere, probably up in the aerie of her room, mistress of all she surveyed from her window, a princess from a fairy tale.

The moon was clear again by the time I reached the mansion. The fire-gutted old structure had an ugly beauty this time of night, like something noble that had been defeated but that still bore dignity.

Another picture of Callie—picking up valuables among the ruins. I hadn't ever even suspected that it was a ruse. That she and Nora were working together to kill Cal.

Callie smiling. Callie laughing. Callie talking to Ham in that strange mixed voice of hers, part pity and part contempt. Not just for Ham, of course. But for all men ultimately.

No lights downstairs. No horses or carriages or wagons out front.

Darkness. Cool after-the-rain silence.

I ground-tied my horse to the east of the place, snatched my rifle and headed for the house.

That was when the guard with the sawed-off chose to come around the far side of the house and stand near the front porch.

He laid his rifle against the steps and rolled himself a cigarette. Then he sat down on the steps and smoked it.

There was likely another guard someplace else.

If I tried going through this guard now, I'd only bring the second around here to the front.

I needed to get in past the guards without alerting Nora I was on my way.

The grass was wet. I slipped a couple of times, landing on my butt.

I worked my way on my haunches to the side door of the mansion, staying in deep shadow. The long muscles in my legs ached already. My boots were soaked from the wet grass.

I reached up and tried the door. Locked. I tried again. Still locked.

I dug out my pocketknife and went to work.

The boys back at Yuma would not have been proud of me. I doubted this was a particularly troublesome lock. But I had no luck with it.

I started sweating so much it got in my eyes. I had to keep wiping my face with my sleeve.

He wore spurs. Otherwise I would never have heard him coming.

Guard number two.

There was a hedge a few feet away. I haunch-walked over to it, gripping my own spurs as I moved. They stayed silent.

I was sure he could hear my breathing. It came in deep searing gasps. As if I was puking up breath.

Deep shadow. Scent of mint from nearby foliage. Sweat. Fear.

His spurs. His sweat. Him spewing a brown stream of chaw.

Him stopping. Right in front of the hedge. Why'd he stop here? Had he heard me? Was he going to start playing games, knowing I was there, taunting me into revealing myself?

I wanted to shoot him but I couldn't. First, because it would tell the other guard and Nora that I was here. Second, because it just wasn't in me.

The Eastern papers always make Westerners sound

as if life doesn't mean much. Well, tell that to the
mother and father who lost their little boy in a corral
accident; or the young wife whose husband died of ty-
phoid; or the elderly wife of the stage guard who got
picked off by bandits for no good reason at all. Ask
them if life doesn't mean much.

Seemed like half an hour went by before he started
moving again.

If he knew I was there, he was taking his time about
letting me know.

And he was sure going about it in a complicated
way.

Because he started walking.

He spat out some more chaw and tightened his grip
on his sawed-off and then he moved to the rear edge of
the house. Then he disappeared.

I gave him a few more minutes.

The stars were low and brilliant. It would be good
sleeping weather, the heat abated this way.

No sound of spurs. Of chaw being spat.

I went back to work on the door.

It took about fifteen minutes.

There were men in Yuma who could have done it in
two.

Because of my baby face, I'd been "kid" to most of
them. But I was a kid in another way, too. I wasn't
skilled in the things most of them were. I drifted into
trouble but I hadn't had the training they had. Most of
them had come from the streets of cities or the dusty

backsides of towns where outlaws liked to hole up. There was a whole community, a whole lexicon, a whole attitude about being a criminal, all of it lost on me.

And that showed up especially in the way I picked locks.

The old-timers used to get a good laugh when they'd see me working on locks. They'd shake their heads and grin at each other. I was glad they found me so hilarious.

Not that I cared much.

My dream in prison had been to meet up with Callie again and marry her and settle down to the straight and honorable life the warden kept talking about in his Sunday sermon.

Yes, Callie was a whore, but that didn't mean she'd be a whore forever.

And yes, I was a train robber, but that didn't mean I'd be a train robber forever, either.

But I wished now that I'd paid more attention to learning about locks in my Yuma years.

Somehow, between certain twists of my knife blade and sheer brute force, I managed to get the door open.

The next thing was to get inside and fast.

I practically dove inside.

I closed the door quietly and then just stood there letting my breath come out in long, hot spasms.

I was on a platform between the first floor and the basement. You could feel the dank coolness of the basement's dirt floor. There'd be a root cellar down there for fruits and vegetables.

I pulled my six-shooter. Got ready to find Nora.

I'd been scared ever since I'd reached the mansion.

But now, thinking of Nora and how she'd killed Callie, I wasn't scared. I was mad. I wanted to hear her tell me some more lies. Especially about Callie.

I went up three steps to the kitchen door. It was open a few inches. I listened. Heard nothing. Pushed the door inward.

The floor was covered in yellow linoleum with big blue wildflowers. The cupboards were done in lacquered oak. The cookstove was massive, a big black iron range with several doors. The icebox was big, too. Oak paneled. Fresh-cut wildflowers sat in vases on top of it so it looked like just another piece of furniture. I saw all this in moonlight. The scent of the last meal—something with stewed beef in it—lingered on the air.

I had to worry about stray glances from the outside. One of the guards passing by a window and glimpsing me.

I moved as swiftly as I could—without bumping into anything—through the dark house.

The dining room was twice—maybe three times—the size of any dining room I'd ever seen before. Easy to imagine powerful men from the Territory eating here, getting soup in their walrus mustaches.

The living room was where they'd have their cigars and brandy afterward. Victorian lamps and overstuffed couches and chairs were grouped around an enormous baby grand piano. The bench overlooked the front grounds. Easy to imagine beautiful Nora there, features made even lovelier by the lamplight, playing serious music for people who'd listen to anything as long as they could watch her play it.

Even in shadow, the winding staircase was dizzying. Its base was wide, and as it rose it narrowed and curved, giving one the sense of ascending into another realm entirely. You expected fog or at least mist as you climbed up. And the cry of lonely and nocturnal animals.

I kept my hand on the banister. I was afraid I'd miss a step in the gloom. I walked carefully.

After I took the second turn on the staircase, I saw a faint light at the edge of the second-floor landing.

The light in Nora's room, no doubt.

When I reached the second floor, I stopped.

The light came from the right side of the huge house. Down at the end of the hall. From a partially opened door.

Humming, then. The voice sweet. Girlish.

I tiptoed. Hugging the wall in case I stumbled. Gun ready.

Sachet. Perfume. Sweet-scented lamp oil. Girl world. Rich girl. A canopy bed, no doubt. Expensive dolls. Books. Expensive prints. I'd seen magazine photographs of how they live. Callie should have been in this world for at least a few days of her life. All poor girls should.

Somewhere in the gloom a grandfather clock tolled the quarter hour.

My heart threatened to tear from my chest. My gun almost fell from my hand. Scared the shit out of me. I was shaking badly. Clock echo continuing for several long seconds.

I was wrong about not being scared. Even my hatred of Nora wasn't enough to overcome my fear. This was a world of wealth and prestige. It shrunk me in every sense. I'd worked here meager as a slave. Nothing had changed. Not all the guns in the world would change it.

The gun led me down the rest of the hall. Still tiptoeing. Still shaking.

Her singing stopped. A faint scratching sound followed. And then the tiny meow of a kitten.

"Oh, Peach," she said, "are you hungry again? I just fed you about an hour ago. If I feed you any more, you'll look like a balloon. A big peach-colored balloon. And then none of the male kittens will want to court you. They like their lady friends to be slender and trim. Just the way you are now. Now, why don't you just sit in my lap and let me brush my hair?"

The scratching was a brush being drawn through chestnut-colored hair that reached her shoulders and framed that elegant, heartbreaking face.

Peach should listen to her. If there was one thing Nora understood, it was beauty and how to use it. Whether it was on a male feline or a male human.

The door wasn't open more than a few inches. To

see anything useful I needed to be on the other side of the door frame.

I needed to know where she was with respect to the door. A night like this, all the trouble, she might well have a gun sitting on her beauty stand. If I came in and couldn't find her right away, she might have time to grab her weapon. Shooting me would be no trouble at all for her.

Somebody came in downstairs. Front door. Heavy footsteps. One of the guards.

Would he be coming up here?

The house was so big his footsteps got lost easily. They were loud, less loud, and gone. From what I could recall of the first floor layout, he was working his way toward the kitchen. At least that was my best guess.

Who knew? Maybe there was a back staircase. These mansions frequently had secret staircases. Maybe he'd figured out I was in here and was coming up to get me.

All I could do was wait.

And then Peach came out. Not far. One, two steps maybe.

Tiny orange tabby. Peering into the overwhelming darkness. So small she could ride the palm of my hand. Scared but curious. Sweet little pink nose.

"Peach!" Nora called. "You stay in here!"

Her running across the bedroom. Door opening. Slender pale hand seizing the kitten just in time.

Dragging the kitten back inside.

I had to make a quick decision. She might close the bedroom door. Meaning I'd have to *open* the door to get in. That would be a problem.

I could spring on her now. If I caught her, I could push her inside. That would be good. But it would also give her time to scream. The guards.

The door started closing. The hallway darkened.

I took the last three steps. In the half-closed doorway, she was commiserating with Peach. Baby talk.

She didn't see me until I was on top of her, knocking Peach from her arms, grabbing her hair, clamping my hand over her mouth. She was all her perfume and sachet. The perfect lady. Even terror didn't spoil her looks.

I'd predicted the appointments of the bedroom pretty well. Right down to the canopy bed. I threw her down on it. Straddled her backside. Kept my hand right on her mouth. Whipped my kerchief from my back pocket. She was gagged tight.

The odd intimacy of it struck me then. I could feel her softly sloping bottom between my legs and the soft hot sweet flesh of her back and arms as I leaned to gag her. Just a few days ago, this would have been a dream moment.

Just a few days ago . . .

There was a plain Shaker chair at the small writing desk in the corner. I grabbed her and dragged her to it. Then I got into the desk. Set out paper and pen.

Peach jumped up on the desk.

I picked her up. Stroked her.

"Didn't mean to scare you."

Nora looked horrified that hands such as mine would touch a creature as sweet and holy as Peach. She'd apparently already forgotten about the brother she'd killed.

I dug into my pocket and brought out the ring. Pushed it into her face.

Her eyes widened in recognition.

"The down payment you gave Callie."

She tried to talk against the gag but it was too tight.

"Ham lived long enough to tell me about it, Nora. Killing your own brother must have been tough, huh? Or maybe not. Maybe you enjoyed it. Callie wanted to back out, didn't she? She was going to do something right for once and you killed her for it."

This time she only muttered against the gag. I tossed the ring on the desktop. She instinctively picked it up, put it in her pocket.

"You're going to write a confession. Make it simple. Just tell them what you did."

I put the six-shooter in her face. Just where the ring had been a few moments earlier.

"I know you're an educated woman, Nora. All you Rutledges are educated. So writing a note like this shouldn't take long at all."

She shook her head.

I lifted her hand. Picked up the pen. Put it in her fingers.

She just sat there staring straight ahead.

"I'd just as soon kill you, Nora. You better keep that in mind."

Staring straight ahead. Silently.

"You think those guards are going to save you? There won't be time. They come after me, I'll take you out first. You better keep that in mind, Nora."

I put the barrel against her temple.

"Now, write, Nora."

She wrote. She must've gone three minutes nonstop. There was a small jar of ink on the desk. She kept dipping her pen. I couldn't see what she was writing. I'd let it be a surprise.

Peach was back up on the desk. I touched her damp little nose. She turned around completely and gave me an exotic view of her little pink flower bud of a butthole. Then she turned around yet again and looked up at me with those imploring blue kitten eyes of hers. Back on the farm I'd had a kitten that I'd sneak in sometimes at night. I learned to sleep on my back because she liked to sleep on my chest. My folks held the farmer belief that no animal but the family dog should be allowed inside. After she got past the mewling stage, she couldn't sleep on my chest anymore. Her meows were too loud and Ma found out about her right away.

She stopped writing.

Set the pen down.

Sat back.

I picked the page up and read it:

> *I was sitting in my room with my cat Peach when this man Sam Conagher broke in here, gagged me, and at gunpoint insisted that I write a "confession" claiming to have killed my own beloved brother, Cal. All I can hope is that my father's guards decide to come inside and save me. Otherwise, I hate to think what he'll do to me before he kills me. I would rather be left to Indians than to this man.* —Nora Rutledge

I laughed and wadded it up and pitched it into the wicker wastebasket.

"You really know how to use that helpless virgin routine."

She glared at me. Muttered something lost against the gag.

"You always make it sound like you just got out of a convent. And men love that. I was so crazy about you I couldn't see what was in plain sight."

I thought of Callie.

"I loved her, Nora. I don't give a damn that you killed Ham and I sure don't give a damn that you killed that punk brother of yours. But I do give a damn that you killed Callie."

She just watched me.

I wanted to slap her.

I leaned forward. Picked up another piece of paper. Put the pen back in her hand.

"Now write a real one."

She shook her head again.

I got up and stretched. My leg muscles were still sore from the kind of walking I'd been doing. I looked around the room.

"You going to make a lot of changes when the old man kicks off and you've got all that money? Yours and Cal's together should be quite a pile. You're gonna be the most powerful woman in the Territory." I smiled at her. "You think people are scared of you now. Wait till you're the boss of all this. They'll be bowing and scraping till their backs give out."

She hadn't written a word.

"Start writing."

She sighed deeply and then leaned toward the desk as if she were going to start writing.

She was a good actress. Knew just how to go convincingly through the motions so I wouldn't be aware of her real intention until it was too late.

She grabbed the ink bottle and hurled it at the window.

It exploded through the glass.

You're on guard outside with a sawed-off and your lonely cigarette and you hear glass breaking like that—what do you think you're going to do?

Peach meowed.

Nora threw herself off the chair and tore her gag free and started screaming.

Another decision.

I could grab her as a hostage and hole up here. Or I could run. The hostage situation presented some opportunities but one big problem. Getting out of a room like this. Even with my gun on her, there were too many ways for them to pick me off when I finally had to leave the room.

Running wouldn't accomplish much—this time I wouldn't have a head start. The guards would be right on me—but it was the only chance of escape I had.

I ran.

The only course for me was down the same steps I'd come up. In the darkness that wasn't easy. I had to get down them and off them as soon as possible. The guards would have an easy time picking me off on the stairs.

They came in the back way.

They sounded like wagon horses exploding through the back door. Shouting. Cursing.

There was a long shadowy open stretch between the bottom step and the front door. If I could make it . . .

But the chances were too great against me. By the furious thundering noise they were making, they were near the front of the house.

I hurried away from the steps, into the hallway that opened just behind me. I'd have to find a room to hide in and then sneak out a window.

The sitting room looked regal, even in the gloom. The furnishings were large and imposing but I didn't see any place that promised to be a good hidey-hole.

I kept going down the hallway.

A maid's room of some kind. Fresh linen. An ironing board. A plump basket of fresh laundry. All silver, thanks to the stream of moonlight through a mullioned window. No place to hide.

Two more doors. A small den, which was no help. And a larger den. A big help.

A leather couch near a window. Perfect for my purposes.

Across the room. Behind the couch. Breath coming in swelling gasps.

Footsteps slapping down the hallway.

Shout: "You go upstairs and see how Miss Nora is! I'll look down here!"

At least I was facing only one man.

He repeated my pattern of quickly opening doors and searching rooms. And had no better luck finding what *he* was looking for.

The window wouldn't open.

I tried it twice and it wouldn't budge.

Slow learner. It wasn't until my third attempt that I realized the mullioned handle had been snapped off somehow. You'd need a pliers or something to open this one.

He was midpoint in the hall.

All the time cursing under his breath. Impressive cursing, too. Eloquent in its way. Couple of words I hadn't heard since prison. Which made me wonder about his background. Rutledge probably wasn't in the practice of hiring saints. What was a small thing like a prison record when you needed a gunny?

I worked my way up to the next window.

He slammed a door. Moved a little closer to the large den.

I got the window open with no trouble.

And that was when I accidentally bumped into a small table. I was swinging my leg up to push myself through the open square of window frame when the rowel of my spur caught the edge of a piece of embroidery that had been placed over the table. The table not only got nudged good and loud, the items that had been sitting on the embroidery got pitched to the floor. Loud enough to wake a dead man.

Certainly loud enough to alert a hired gun on the prowl.

He heard me and instantly came running.

No time to make it through the window. The frame wasn't all that wide. Thin as I was I could still get hung up there.

I pitched myself to the floor. Rolled under a large table.

I had to cover my mouth. My gasping sounded loud as drums.

He came charging into the room. I could hear him and smell him and see him from about the top of his Texas boots down.

He said, "Make this easy for both of us, friend. Just slide your gun out on the floor and we won't have no trouble. You don't get hurt and I don't get hurt. I got a sweet little grandma in Missouri I'd like to see again before I die."

This was definitely a higher caliber of gunny.

Your average gunny would've just told me to come out with my hands up or he'd fill me with lead. Or some other line of melodrama he'd picked up in a dime novel out there in the bunkhouse all those lonesome cowboy nights.

This one had a sweet little grandma.

I shot him in the leg.

He didn't make much noise. He mostly swore at me. He made the mistake of reaching down to about midcalf where I'd shot him. Wanted to touch his wound. See just how bad it was as he hobbled away for cover. And that was when I shot him in the hand. It wasn't his gun hand but it would do.

I crawled from beneath the table. He had turned and was sort of haunch-walking over behind another couch. He was moving slow and clumsy. I jumped him. I didn't want to kill him. He hadn't tried to kill me. But I did need to put him out for a while.

I jumped on his back.

He tried to throw me off but I hit him three times very hard in the side of his head with my fist. He sprawled flat beneath me. The calf wound, the hand wound and now the pounding on his head had put him out for a time.

I grabbed his gun in case he revived earlier than I wanted him to.

I could hear the other one coming down the stairs. He must have been lighter and younger than this one. He sounded as if he was taking the steps two or three at a time.

Another voice behind him: "Be careful, Scotty. He's a very treacherous man."

Nora, of course. Calling *me* treacherous.

I waited for Scotty behind the door. He came in smartly and confidently. He wasn't running now. He was striding.

When he got to the threshold of the door, I got myself ready. As soon as he was inside, I'd fling the door away and jump him. Then I'd throw him down next to his partner.

I couldn't figure out what he was waiting for. Why the hell didn't he just walk into the den?

I found out soon enough.

He pushed the barrel of his Colt between door edge and frame and said, "I figured that's where you'd be."

His gun was pointing directly at me.

"Shit," I said.

"Put the gun down."

What choice did I have?

"Or I'll fill you with lead."

So *he* was the one reading the dime novels.

I leaned down as far as I could to put my gun on the floor.

"Slow and easy, gunny-boy."

More dime novel.

I did it fast. It was my only hope.

He'd been clever using the door against me. Now I was going to try and be clever using the door right back against *him*.

When I flung the door open, it caught the barrel of

his gun. The gun was stuck between door edge and frame.

By the time he'd retrieved it, I had my gun back and was diving for cover. I rolled behind the desk that took up a good share of the west end of the room.

He wasted no time. He used his sawed-off.

He apparently thought he knew where I was so he came in blasting.

But I wasn't there, so I had time to blast back.

I got him in both knees. The funny thing was, his first inclination was to go over backwards. Then he righted himself and did it the predictable way. He crumbled to the floor, a puppet suddenly without knees for support.

She was screaming again.

But this didn't seem to be general-purpose screaming. This seemed to have a purpose.

The sound of the horses then overwhelmed her screams.

I ran to the window.

The second guard was still conscious and fired at me. He shattered the window I was gaping out of. The bullet missed me but did a good job of covering me in glass shards that sparkled diamond-like in the moonlight. An angle of glass stabbed deep into my shoulder.

The yard was filled with men.

Rutledge and his boys were back.

They'd obviously heard the shot and were already rushing toward the mansion.

Chapter 16

I held out for half an hour.

I tried to hoard my ammunition but hoarding wasn't possible when I had to respond to every gunny who came at me.

Rutledge himself went around and lit all the lamps in the den. Daring me to shoot him. I declined the honor. I had nothing against him. He'd been betrayed here as much as I'd been.

When he was through with the lamps, and the room glowed with a friendly golden warmth that belied the tension and gunplay, he stood in the center of the parquet floor and said, with a great deal of weariness, "Let's just get it over with, Conagher. We're going to hang you and you know we're going to hang you. Your friend the sheriff should never have let you go." He cleared his throat. He still sounded tired. "I want the satisfaction of hanging you, Conagher. I've told my men that they have permission to wound you but any man who kills you will die himself. By my hand. So you can make it easy on yourself or you can get wounded before we hang you. But either way, we *are* going to hang you."

I wanted to ask him how Earl was. But somehow I couldn't find my voice. I was all crouched up behind the leather couch. I kept counting my bullets. I guess I was hoping that they'd magically multiplied.

The end of my life was at hand. You always wonder when and how it's going to happen, and when it finally *does* happen, you're surprised. Trapped behind a couch. Dirty, dejected, hungry, tired. I felt like the sorriest man on earth. But then I thought of Callie, and Corrina, whose Earl had probably died helping me escape. And their kids. And then I didn't feel so bad.

After that, Rutledge didn't say anything. He just went over and sat down in a leather wingback chair. He crossed his long legs and sat with his chin in his hand, staring off. It was as if he were utterly alone. It was pretty easy to guess he was thinking about Cal. He'd hardly been the ideal son, but you forget things like that when he dies.

I wondered what he was up to. I soon found out.

They were smart. They moved on me from both sides.

And they timed it well.

Just when I'd started to relax a little—there hadn't

been any talk or any action for several minutes—they came.

The two in front distracted me with gunfire while the one in back, climbing up through the smashed-out window, waited his turn. When he was sure the two in front had me nailed down, he dove through the window, got me around the neck and wrestled me to the floor.

One of the front ones smashed his boot heel on my hand. My gun skittered free, twirled under the couch.

They dragged me to the center of the room, to where Rutledge sat in his chair. Exhausted emperor in expensive cattleman's town outfit. He'd dropped his Stetson on the floor next to the chair.

He stood up then. I'd forgotten how much taller than me he was. There was a sadness in his eyes that vanished quickly. Replaced by fury.

He spat at me. He was practiced in the art. His spittle hung from my forehead and the tip of my nose.

Then he slapped me.

But even with an open hand there was so much thunder that I could feel my teeth loosen under the blow. Blood started running from the insides of my cheeks.

He wasn't done yet.

He grabbed the front of my hair with his left hand and smashed his right fist into my face once, twice, three times.

Nobody said anything. They just watched. Listened.

He didn't say anything even then. He just nodded to

one of the men. The man left the room quickly. I understood the significance of the nod. The man was getting the rope. The man was preparing the tree limb.

"You killed my son."

It wasn't easy to speak. Blood was filling my mouth.

"No, I didn't, sir. Your daughter did."

"You killed my son and now I'm going to kill you."

It was as if I hadn't said anything at all. So ridiculous an accusation that it hadn't even registered in his mind.

He wanted to kill me with his own hands. That would have been the preferred method. But he wanted the cachet of legality. Even lynching wasn't better than simply beating a man to death. He also wanted to curse me. He was shaking. His whole body. His face was bloodred. He wanted to curse me but he couldn't find words vile enough or furious enough to express his rage. I almost felt sorry for him.

"Nora killed Cal."

"If you say that again, I'll kill you right here on the spot."

"It's the truth. She wanted his half of the inheritance. She planned it all out with Callie and Ham. It was all her idea. She came to them. And they were stupid enough to go along with it. Except at the end. Callie backed out. Nora was afraid Callie would go to Earl and tell him everything. So she killed her."

He didn't even try to kill me on the spot.

He just glared at me and said, "I've got a friend

who's a warden. He tells me that right before they hang them most prisoners come up with a whopper of a story. How they're really innocent and all that. But this is pitiful, Conagher. It really is. Dragging in a poor girl like Nora. After she's lost her brother and everything. I pity you, Conagher. I really do. You're a true wretch. I'm doing you a favor by hanging you."

He looked at his men.

"Let's go outside."

I don't know how long it took, getting everything ready for the hanging.

The man working on the rope was having some trouble getting everything fixed up right. He was working with a good-sized oak limb to the near west of the house. Setting up a noose looks easy enough. But it actually takes some know-how and skill.

"Get him on his horse."

While they were waiting for the tree to be set up properly, they decided to get me in *my* proper place.

In all, there were probably twenty, twenty-five men. A few carried wind-whipped torches. Most just stood and watched, smoking cigarettes. The yelling and the shouting and the threatening had all been for town consumption, apparently. They were quiet out here.

"What the hell's taking so long?" Rutledge snapped to the noose man.

"Just about got 'er."

"That's the third time you've said that."

"Well, this time it's true. I've just about got 'er."

"You'd damned well better."

Rutledge came over to my horse. "How's this coming?"

"Fine, Mr. Rutledge," said one of the men.

And from his point of view, it was. They'd bound my wrists and had just now blindfolded me and sat me straight in my saddle. I was all ready to drop down the long dark chute.

Nothing. Blackness. The kerchief around my eyes kept everything dark. My own sweat. My cold bowels.

"If you're going to make your peace with the Lord," Rutledge said, "I'd suggest you do it now."

"You're treating him better than he deserves, Father."

The voice. So simple and sweet. Earnest. Untroubled by the devious ways of the hard harsh world. Innocent.

"I just want to get this over with."

For all that he hated me, there was no pleasure in his voice. At another time I would have admired that. To him he was simply carrying out the law. Nothing more, nothing less.

Around the edges of my blindfold light danced now. Torchlight. The horses neighed and stamped but the men were silent.

I would see Callie soon. I'd never thought much about heaven or hell. Didn't know if I believed in them. But maybe there was something beyond death, beyond even the simplistic notions of heaven and hell.

I sensed I would be with Callie again anyway. In some form. In some realm. Soon.

"Make sure the knot is right," Rutledge said.

"Yessir."

"I want it clean."

"Yessir."

Everyone has seen hangings that don't go right. Where the rope is set at a bad angle and the knot doesn't snap the neck. Where the man suffers and strangles and dangles.

A man came up alongside me. I could smell him and his horse. I could smell the night, the kerosene in the torches, the sweet hay-filled horse shit from the barns.

The man examined the knot. His knuckles were rough against my neck. He smelled of whiskey and cigarettes. "It looks good, Mr. Rutledge."

"Good. Then let's get on with it, Les." Les was apparently the ranch foreman.

To me: "You have anything to say, Conagher?"

"I didn't kill your son. Nora did."

A long pause. I heard him walk closer.

"You're going to die, son," Rutledge said. "Right here and right now. You want your last words to be a lie?"

Again I sensed the odd kindness in the man. For a land baron, he was a pretty decent man.

"Just hang him, Father. Please. I just keep thinking of poor Cal."

Rutledge said, "Get ready to swat the horse."

Swat the horse out from under me. With any luck
I'd have the clean death Rutledge wanted me to have.

"Ready any time you are, sir," said the man behind
me.

I was thinking of Callie again. In the church those
times. At the communion rail. Praying that she'd
change. And crying so hard afterward. It should have
worked out for us. All the cheap things she'd accumu-
lated in her time. Nothing that was good or lasting. I
could see her wearing the ring Nora had given her. The
most expensive piece of jewelry Callie had ever
owned, scratching her initials into it like a possessive
little girl afraid the bogeyman might steal it at night—

"The ring!" I said.

"What?" Rutledge said.

"Nora put a ring in her pocket. An emerald. It was
her mother's. It's there now."

"What's he talking about, Nora?"

I wished I could see. I wanted to rip my blindfold
off.

"Nora gave her the ring so Callie would help her
kidnap and kill your son. Get the ring from Nora and
look inside. Callie scratched her initials in there. CC.
Just ask Nora for the ring."

"You gave your mother's ring away?" Rutledge
said. "That belongs to the family, Nora. No one else.
Now, let me see it."

He was angry over the ring. He would not yet face
the implications of what the ring signified about his
daughter.

"Father, please. Can't you see what he's doing?"

"The ring, Nora."

"He's just buying time for himself. That's all. He tried to steal the ring from my room. That's the only reason he knows about it."

"If that's true, then that woman's initials won't be inside. Now, let me have the ring."

The rolling night silence again, cut only here and there with horse sound and man sound, the occasional cough, the occasional sigh.

I hated my blindness.

In a much quieter voice: "Give me the ring, Nora."

"He's lying, Father."

"The ring. Now."

"You'll always remember this, Father. I'll see that you will. The night you took the word of a killer over mine."

Almost sadly now: "The ring."

Rustle of clothing. I could picture her reaching into the pocket of her dress. Lovely face resentful. "Here," she said, "take it. You wanted it so damned badly."

She started to cry.

I could picture him, too. Holding the ring up to the light. Hoping that he wouldn't find the CC initials there.

His sigh was loud and long.

The initials were there, of course. And now he'd have to face their implications.

He said quietly: "The man they called Ham, Conagher. He was part of it, too?"

"Yes, sir, he was."

"But you weren't?"

"No, sir."

"And Earl wasn't?"

"No, sir. Your daughter and Ham and Callie. But Callie backed out."

"And that's when Nora killed her?"

"Yes, sir."

Another long silence.

Then: "You men head to the bunkhouse for the night. But get Conagher down from that horse first."

"I'm not sure I'd believe him, sir," said one of the men.

"I didn't ask what you think," he said.

"Yessir."

Most of the men slowly turned their horses toward the bunkhouse. I could hear the man working the rope down from the branch. Then he came up beside me. I angled my head. He got the rope off. Even in that little time, my neck had been chafed.

I took the blindfold off myself.

The man slung the rope across his saddle horn and then worked his horse to the distant lights of the bunkhouse.

Leaving me, Rutledge and Nora standing in the moonlight next to the hanging tree.

"Get up to the house, Nora," Rutledge said quietly.

"It's like Les said, Dad. You shouldn't believe him. You really shouldn't." She was still crying gently.

"Saddle up one of the horses in the corral," Rutledge said to me, "and get the hell off my land."

I took a final look at Nora. I didn't want her to be beautiful, but she was. Always. What she'd done should have made her ugly, but I guess there wasn't anything that could make that possible.

"I wish I'd never set eyes on you," Nora said to me. "You're a devil. Deep down in your soul you're a devil."

I went to the barn and got a saddle and then went on down to the corral and got me a pinto. I was just swinging up into the saddle when the shots came.

There were three of them. Two the first time. And then a few seconds later a single one.

It wasn't hard to picture what had happened, though I tried not to. It was funny. I'd actually liked Rutledge and in a strange way I liked him even more now. The ministers always tell you that taking your own life is a sin. But sometimes a man of honor realizes that to live would be a dishonorable thing, like a ship's captain where something terrible occurred. It's your watch. You're ultimately responsible. You do the only thing you can.

The men were walking up to the house. Not running. None of them was eager to get inside. Neither was I.

I fell in next to Les.

"You think he did it?" I said.

"Oh, he did it all right. You didn't hear the shots?"

"I heard them. I thought maybe he was just trying to scare her."

"He never bluffed. Not Mr. Rutledge. That's why people respected him."

When we got to the steps of the house, he said, "Your friend Earl should be here for this. He's the law and all."

"Maybe this was one time Rutledge bluffed. Maybe nothing happened."

He looked at me funny. I'll never forget that look. "You like to dream, don't you, kid?"

We went up the steps and inside. The men from the bunkhouse weren't far behind.

There was a silence such as I'd never heard before. A deep absence of all sound. Not even footsteps could be heard.

Les glanced at me. He seemed to be experiencing the same thing. He made the sign of the cross. And broke the silence.

"He raised me. My old man rode fence for him, and when my folks died in a flood, Rutledge raised me. He was a good man." He was fighting tears.

"Yes, he was," I said.

"You go in and look, all right?"

I nodded. And went deep into the house.

They were both in the sitting room. Nora had fallen onto the couch when he'd killed her, one bullet in the forehead, one in the heart. As for himself, he'd put the gun in his mouth and taken off a hefty chunk of the left side of his head.

"Son of a bitch," Les said. "Son of a bitch." He'd come in right behind me after all.

"That's how he handled things," another man said. "Something wrong, he took care of it."

"Well, he sure took care of this," someone else said.

"Didn't waste no time about it, either," said a third.

Les looked at me. "She really kill her brother?"

"Yeah."

"He was an asshole but he sure didn't have that coming."

"No," I said. "No, he didn't."

"His own daughter," another man said.

"I always wanted to fuck her," said one of the men.

Another laughed and said, "Here's your chance."

Les said, "You men shut up."

The two who'd made the joke shut up like schoolboys who'd just been chastised.

"I'll be headin' out," I said.

"How come?"

"Jinx town. That's what it feels like to me now. I don't want to go back there."

Les smiled bitterly. "You get the jinx feelin' on you, you can't shake it, can you?"

"I can't, anyway."

"Horse is yours, mister."

"Appreciate it."

Another ten minutes and I was gone. I rode beneath the tree where they were going to hang me. And then I spurred the horse hard. I wanted to get away from this part of the Territory as fast as I could.

I rode all night. I didn't want to stop. I was afraid to stop. I just wanted to ride and ride and ride to some storybook land where Callie was still alive and where I wouldn't be cursed with all those foolish damned dreams and schemes of mine. Some storybook world where Earl wouldn't go on a tear and beat up his step kid and where Rutledge wouldn't feel obliged to kill his very own daughter. Some storybook world I'd thought I'd find when I left Kansas so long, long ago.

I rode till dawn and came upon a town with a church. I went in, beat and grubby and sore, and lit a candle for Callie. Then I knelt there for a long time and tried to say a prayer that meant something, but just the old dead rote words came. The prayer meant nothing at all. I stared for a long time at the beautiful blue glow of Callie's candle. And then I went outside and got on my horse and started riding again. Riding fast. To nowhere.

No one knows the American West better.

JACK BALLAS

❏ *THE HARD LAND*   0-425-15519-6/$4.99

❏ *BANDIDO CABALLERO*
                                    0-425-15956-6/$5.99

❏ *GRANGER'S CLAIM*
                                    0-425-16453-5/$5.99

The Old West in all its raw glory.